Xmas 1998

from Linda

THE NERISSA CLAIRE CASE

Carla Brent is charged with the first-degree murder of her husband, and the case against her is damning. She is known to have been jealous about his affair with a go-go dancer, Nerissa Claire, and Carla was found gun in hand, beside her husband's corpse. Her story is that a masked stranger shot him and thrust the gun into her hand. In some despair, her lawyer wants to produce Nerissa in court and plead manslaughter, though Carla is aggressively refusing any plea but 'not guilty'. However, Nerissa had disappeared....

THE NERISSA CLAIRE CASE

THE NERISSA CLAIRE CASE

by
Hillary Waugh

MAGNA PRINT BOOKS
Long Preston, North Yorkshire,
England.

British Library Cataloguing in Publication Data.

Waugh, Hillary,
    The Nerissa Claire case.
    I. Title
    813'.54(F)

    ISBN 1-85057-440-5
    ISBN 1-85057-441-3 Pbk

First Published in Great Britain by Victor Gollancz Ltd. 1983

Published in Large Print 1989 by arrangement with Victor
Gollancz Ltd. London and the copyright holder.

Printed and bound in Great Britain by
Redwood Burn Limited, Trowbridge, Wiltshire.

CHAPTER ONE

He was totally hairless, stood six-feet-five and looked like an undernourished chicken. His beak could dig kernels out of the barnyard, his stringy neck had wattles, and his shirt collar was twice the size of his throat.

That doesn't mean he was to laugh at. He may have looked like a cartoon, but he oozed money, and money isn't funny. He wore the smell of it like cologne. His suit would buy my bedroom suite, and the look he gave my office suggested fumigators.

From the hang of his clothes and the width of his collar, I, being a reasonably smart detective, could deduce he'd lost a lot of weight recently. I could also wonder if his family might not be measuring him for a pine box and second-guessing his will.

This didn't seem to worry him much, for he carried a gold-headed cane that could crack a skull and handled it like a country club pro adrift with his driver. What he played down, and what I noticed most, was a pair of X-ray eyes that made me feel I should go to confession.

Eileen led him in like a Seeing Eye dog. Eileen, if you don't know, is my secretary. She's sharp, shrewd, competent, gorgeous and very female. Her figure would stand you on your wig, but she won't show it to you, except just enough to make you pant. And she knows exactly where too much is enough. TV producers would make a sex symbol out of her on a three-day promotion budget, except that TV producers don't come to private detectives— at least not looking for talent. And she doesn't haunt their haunts. For some strange reason she's content to be a secretary to a private detective and coax potential clients into my inner sanctum.

As for this gaunt totem pole she brought through the door, she'd briefed me on him in advance. His name was Leonard Hargrove Wood, he was a lawyer, and she showed me an embossed card, which bore his name, the words, ATTORNEY-AT-LAW and, in a quiet corner, 'Public Defender.'

Public defenders, for your information, get scale wages for representing accused felons who don't have any money. If Leonard Hargrove Wood had spent his legal lifetime in that backwater area, he should have been wearing

Good Will discards, not toting gold-headed canes.

Eileen was tender with him. She handed him into the customer chair like the Easter Bunny delivering an egg, and she gave me a merry smile when she went away. She knew an embossed public-defender's card was a contradiction that made Leonard Hargrove Wood a mystery, and she believed private detectives were put on earth to solve mysteries.

I fondled his card, and a passing truck filled the room with a growl. It was a hot June morning, and the windows were wide in hopes of a breeze. What came in was soot and sound. 'Mr Wood?'

Mr Wood twitched a corner of his mouth. An air-conditioner was his idea of proper noise. 'I'll come to the point,' he said, as if eager to be gone. 'How good are you at finding people?'

I gave the stock answer. 'That depends on whom you want found.'

'Whom?' He eyed me anew. 'A literate detective?'

'Not really. My fourth-grade teacher was a bug on grammar.'

He remained impressed. I could have been teaching Shakespeare at Yale. 'The "whom" in this case,' he went on slowly, 'is a very attractive and elusive young woman by the name of Nerissa Claire. She shares—or shared —a rented condominium with a cousin named Shelly Polk, who's come east to attend modelling school. Nerissa left the condominium two weeks ago, ostensibly to get married. At least that's what Miss Polk says. Miss Polk, however, does not know whom she meant to marry or where she went.' Leonard Wood spread long thin hands. 'Does the prospect of finding her appeal to you, Mr Kaye?'

'Of course. That's my business.' (What did he expect me to say?)

'It might not be an easy task. There isn't much to go on.'

'The longer it takes, the more it'll cost,' I said. 'If there comes a time when I don't think the job can be done, I'll tell you.'

'Money isn't an object,' Mr Wood replied, and from the look of his clothes, I could believe him. If he wanted me soaking wet, he could buy a lake to dunk me in.

I pulled over a pad and pencil. 'Then we might as well get at it. What does she look like? Do you have a picture?'

He shook his head. 'No, no picture. Her cousin says she's brunette, about five-feet-four, with a good figure. Does that help?'

'No. How old is she?'

'Young, I believe. Twenties.'

'Background? Where's she from? What're her parents' names?'

Mr Wood didn't have that information, either. 'But it doesn't matter. Her cousin says Nerissa left home six years ago and hasn't been back.'

'Occupation?'

Mr Wood said with distaste. 'She was a go-go dancer.'

'Whereabouts?'

'A place called Frank's Bar. But they can't tell you anything. I've already been there. She quit two weeks ago.'

I put down my pencil and sat back. Leonard Hargrove Wood didn't smell of money anymore, he stank of fishiness. How come an aged public defender wore those elegant clothes? How come a lawyer his age could be so easily conned by the missing girl's cousin, a child even by my standards? And why was he coming to me with this song and dance? Did he think I was some kind of patsy?

I guess I looked insulted, for he stared at me with a genuinely baffled expression on his plucked-chicken face. 'Frank's Bar is on La-Verne Street,' he said, trying to reassure me. 'But I've been there. I've been trying to track down Nerissa Claire myself.'

The poor guy wasn't trying to con me. He

11

was just naïve.

'Mr Wood,' I said, slowly and carefully. 'I presume you are protecting a client's interest, that this girl has fleeced some unsuspecting, very well-to-do male out of a great deal of money and has now retired to a newly purchased villa in southern France, southern Italy or Argentina, and this well-to-do male, who is probably a close friend of yours, wants you to help him find her and get back some of what he's given her. And you, being loyal and true, are trying to accomplish the mission without revealing any information that might be traced back to, and embarrass, your friend.'

I leaned elbows on my desk. 'But I have to tell you, Mr Wood, forget it. Such a woman can't be traced without pictures, without description, without knowledge of her occupation, habits, friends, relatives—all the things that connect her to her environment. These are the railroad tracks that take her from here to there, and she can't be traced without tracks,' I stood up. 'I can't find this girl with what you tell me about her. I'm not a magician. You don't tell me you want the queen of hearts and I cut the deck and there she is. And I can assure you that no other private detective is a magician either. Some might tell you they are, and you're welcome to go to them and see.'

Mr Wood sat for long seconds assimilating my message. Ultimately, he reached a conclusion. 'Mr Kaye,' he said. 'I believe you think I'm a fraud.'

'That's one of the possibilities.'

He smoothed both hands over his bald pate as if recharging batteries, and gave me a frostbitten smile. 'My clothes, my card, my occupation, my complaint? They don't make sense to you?'

I sat back down and showed I was listening.

He went on, still smoothing his scalp. 'That story you just told me, about the wealthy man who'd been fleeced by a gold digger and wanted me to help him recoup—that's very good. It dawned on me as you told it that it was a most logical conclusion for a detective to reach, given the clues at hand.'

He pressed his fingertips together at his chest, and his smile thawed a degree or two. 'Suppose I told you I went to law school when I was fifty? What would you say to that?'

'I'd say, "Go on." '

He waited until a couple more trucks grumbled and rumbled through the street and their sounds had faded away. Then he said, 'Suppose a banker who's hated banking reaches the point at age fifty when he can do what he's always wanted to do—become a lawyer? Suppose he struggles through law school in the company of students one half his age, and suppose he achieves his great objective—he gets a law-school degree and passes his bar exams!

'Picture a man in that situation, Mr Kaye. What is he going to do with that precious privilege of practising law in this fair state?

'Can he go into business for himself. Who would be the first customer of someone my age? Can he be hired by a successful law firm? They want twenty-five-year-old talent, not fifty-five-year-old. They want lawyers with a long life span ahead of them.

'What you find is that about the only thing an old new-lawyer can do is become a public defender. The pay is minimal and the attraction is equally minimal. Lawyers with ability only serve when they're drafted—like civilians doing jury duty. Any lawyer who becomes a public defender by choice is either someone dedicated to the cause of the poor, or, more likely, so inept that he couldn't do better on his own.'

He held up an admonishing hand. 'And there's one other case. There's the lawyer like me, who doesn't need money, who doesn't have any love for this field of law but who has no other choice. The only way I can practice law is by defending the hapless and fundless whom the court appoints me to defend. That has become my calling.' He smiled a sardonic smile. 'So you see, you're quite wrong about my purpose here. I'm not trying to help a rich friend who's been indiscreet. I'm really trying to help a poor woman who's guilty of murder.'

CHAPTER TWO

Since I looked at him encouragingly, Leonard Wood recharged his batteries with some more pate stroking and gave me a more hospitable smile. 'Tell me, Mr Kaye. Are you familiar with the Carla Brent murder case?'

It didn't ring any bells. 'No.'

'Carla Brent, poor woman, committed the unpardonable crime of killing her husband.' Mr Wood's head bowed a little. He lifted it again. 'That is not to say that her husband didn't *deserve* killing. He did. Carla was as justified in her act of passion as any person could ever be justified for the commission of any crime. Her husband was a loathsome, despicable, unwholesome wretch.'

15

He was shifting into third gear about now. I said, 'It was over another woman?'

His eyes gleamed. 'Yes, yes. Then you *have* heard of the case!'

'No,' I answered. 'Just crimes of passion. And Nerissa Claire is the other woman in this case?'

'Yes! That's right!' Wood gave me a gold star. 'You're making headway!'

'And you're starting to give me some information.'

'I am?'

'Not much, but some. Keep it up.'

Mr Wood crossed one expensively trousered leg over the other. 'Well, I might as well tell you the whole thing. It's no secret. It's been in all the papers for the past two weeks. Her husband was a police officer, and there was a big brouhaha in the department when this broke out.'

That's when I realized I *had* heard about it. 'Matthew Brent,' I said. 'Executive secretary to the chief of police, a ten-year veteran!'

'That's right. You know him?'

'No, I don't know him. I only read that his wife killed him.' I reappraised Leonard Hargrove Wood. 'You're defending the wife!'

Leonard Hargrove Wood pressed his fingertips together, pleased at being recognized. 'A

16

logical deduction,' he said. 'Matthew Brent was the wage earner. His wife took care of the home. His wife has never been in the work force. She has no skills. She has no money. Unless I can get a proper plea for her, she'll be destitute. She'll never see a cent of what her dead husband is worth.'

Now I was on the right wavelength. 'And your proper plea for her is manslaughter? You're not going to plead her not guilty?'

He smiled wolfishly. 'You understand,' he said. 'A not guilty plea is out of the question. After all, she did it. So it's a matter of what else is available. The charge against her is murder in the first degree. The district attorney will drop it to murder in the second degree if she'll plead guilty and save a trial. But there's no gain for her in that. The sentence in both cases is life imprisonment, with parole after twenty years. Either way she'd come out of prison twenty years older and without a cent to her name. She'd be free, but destitute.'

I said, 'So you'll go for manslaughter in hopes of a short sentence—maybe a suspended sentence. And if it's manslaughter, she can collect her husband's benefits—life insurance...'

'Quite right.' The smile broadened and his eyes glistened, but they were looking past me,

17

staring into the triumph of that verdict. That would give the old newly crowned lawyer a big future all right: 'Go ahead and kill your husband. I'll get you off with all your widow's benefits besides.' He'd have to turn the clients away.

But that was his business. I said to him, 'What do you want with Nerissa Claire? Was she a witness to the killing?'

He shook his head. 'Nerissa Claire was go-go dancing when Carla put six bullets into her husband. That was in their bedroom at ten-thirty on the evening of June first...two weeks ago today.'

'Does she have information pertinent to your plea? Is she willing to back up the wife?'

Mr Wood made a harsh, guttural sound of sudden anger. 'I'm sure she wouldn't lift a finger to help the wife. The wife was her rival. The wife ended her cosy setup by killing her lover. In fact, while her cousin claims Nerissa said she left to get married, I think it more likely that she disappeared just so she couldn't get dragged into this mess. The night he was killed was the night she quit.'

'She was told about it at work?'

'That I don't know. The manager only told me she quit.'

I shook my head. 'Then what do you want

Nerissa for? She's going to be a hostile witness.'

He gave me a bemused smile. He had a plan in mind. 'I don't care *what* her attitude is,' he said. 'In fact, the worse she behaves, the better. I want to put her up on that witness stand as an example.'

'Example?'

'I want to show her off as a sexy bitch. I want to show her as a home wrecker, as somebody the wife couldn't compete with. I want the jury to understand how desperate a wife would feel when she's got a Nerissa Claire working against her.'

'You'd better work for an all-female jury,' I warned him. 'The males might fall for her line.'

'I'm going to pack that jury with as many women as I can,' he answered. 'Homely women, married women, insecure women. If I don't get a manslaughter verdict, I'll damned well get a hung jury.'

I stroked my chin and stared at the window. Another truck went by, and there was the sound of a siren. My office is on a busy street.

Inside the room there was silence. He was waiting, and I was pondering. He grew impatient. 'I've been frank with you, Mr Kaye, I've given you my game plan. That's because I'm under the impression that the client relation-

19

ship with a private detective has the same confidentiality as the relationship between a client and his lawyer, between a parishioner and his priest.'

'Of course,' I told him. 'That goes without saying. That's not what I'm thinking about.'

'If you disapprove of my scheme...'

I waved a hand. 'I'm not a judge, I'm a detective. You want me to do a job. If I think I can, I accept and you become my client. If I don't think I can deliver, I tell you goodbye and wish you luck. If I know somebody who can do what I can't, I give you his card—except that I'm an arrogant sonuvabitch and I won't admit there's anybody in the business who can do a job I can't do.'

His thick lips formed a tight line. 'And you're telling me you don't think this woman can be found?'

I shook my head. 'You didn't hear me right. I said you can't expect a private detective to cut a deck of cards to the queen of hearts—not without clues. You told me you couldn't give me any clues. But now you're giving me some.'

Since he had no eyebrows, all I can say is he raised the skin above his eyes. 'I am?'

'You're telling me she's a home wrecker. You're telling me she wrecks middle-class homes. You're telling me she's content with a life-style cops can support, not U.S. senators, munitions manufacturers, or the country-club set.

'And the betrayed wife kills the husband instead of the other woman! That's another interesting tidbit.'

Leonard Hargrove Wood smiled broadly, and on his face a smile was scary. You got the feeling he had secret knowledge that the roof beams were buckling.

'I'm not saying,' I quickly added, 'that you've given me anything that will help me locate her. I'm only saying that you know more about her than you think you do.'

His smile didn't let up. He wasn't hearing me, he was watching me. He rose and held out his long stringy hand. 'You'll take the case?'

I didn't accept the hand. I didn't really accept *him*. But I'm hardheaded (boneheaded, if you want the truth) and I wouldn't give him a blunt no. What I said was, 'If you'll arrange for me to talk to Carla Brent, give me Miss Polk's address and the place where Nerissa go-go danced, and if you give my secretary a thousand-dollar certified cheque on account, I'll take a look around. The thousand won't last very long, so I'll let you know when I need more.'

I half hoped that would stop him. I half

hoped he'd decide I was a money-grubbing bastard who wanted to take him for a ride. I thought he'd turn on his heel, give me his A-plus sneer and tell me he was taking his business to my most dangerous competitor.

As usual, I was wrong. He produced a wallet as thick as a first edition of *Vanity Fair* and pulled out ten one-hundred-dollar bills. (God knows how many more were in there.) He dropped them on my desk like so much chaff and exclaimed with relief that now his problems were solved. He was already seeing me producing his star witness, and seeing her absolve his client. And he was seeing himself proving to the world that it pays to kill unwanted husbands, that you can murder for fun and profit. Just come to Leonard Hargrove Wood when you get arrested. Come and bring money.

I counted the hundred-dollar bills. There wasn't anything else to do. He scribbled addresses on my pad and beamed his man-eating smile. 'When do you want to see Carla?' he asked.

We settled on two o'clock that afternoon in one of the interview rooms at the jail. He said he'd meet me there, and I walked him through the outer office and showed him out the door. When I shut it behind me, Eileen shook her head. 'He looks loaded and you look unhappy.

The two don't add up. You *did* get hired, didn't you? He acted as if he'd come to the right place.'

I said, 'Sometimes something called scruples gets in my way—not enough to trip over, mind you, just enough to catch in my hair.'

She said, soberly, 'Who does he want you to cheat?'

'If you'd said whom instead of who, he'd have hired you too.'

'Fly that around again, will you? I was counting sheep.'

'What he wants me to do,' I told her, 'is help him get a cop killer off on a manslaughter charge. Never mind that the cop killer was the cop's wife, and it was over another woman, not in the line of duty. I was a cop myself once and I'm prejudiced.'

'And that's not what's bothering you either. That has nothing to do with scruples.'

'That's right. What it boils down to is, I don't like to see one human being kill another human being and profit by the act, especially when aided and abetted by our justice system. And this is what this damned new client is paying me to help him do.

'On the other hand, he's entitled to do everything for his client that the law allows, and he'd be derelict if he didn't. So if he asks

23

me to help him, I have to. On the other hand, I don't *want* to. But to say that is to be judgmental, and I'm not the judge. So I have to do what I can.'

Eileen said, 'You know what your problem is? You have a conscience.'

'If I do, it has a helluva time trying to determine what's right and what's wrong.'

'Who doesn't?'

I made a face at her on my way back to my office, and she blew me a kiss.

CHAPTER THREE

The jail, which goes by the name Retention Centre, to please the sociologists, occupies a city block half a mile from the centre of town and is a large, convoluted complex of bricks and barred windows. Despite what they call it, it looks like a J-A-I-L. I mean, it has that glowering, forbidding appearance that says, 'You won't like it here.'

Inside the door, off the macadam parking lot that covered erstwhile lawns and gardens, is a small anteroom presided over by a guy behind

24

a window who wants to know your business. He checked my name and buzzed the lock, which passed me through to a barren, well-worn waiting room, where Leonard Wood was sitting on a bench, watching me with cobra eyes.

There was an armed guard against the far door who went off at a signal from the laywer to summon the prisoner while Leonard shook my hand and asked if I wanted him present during my interview with Carla Brent. I said I'd rather form my own impressions and we could compare notes later. He said he'd wait for me there and sat down on the bench again. Some lawyers have things to do. This one didn't.

When the guard returned, he led me through a long corridor that needed light and paint to the visiting rooms. They were cubicles with a table and a couple of benches in each, a small window at the back and a barred door in front. Carla Brent was in the first one, sitting at a table, with a female guard at the door. Carla Brent was a dark, spare woman nearly six feet tall, with a sullen, angular face and a figure too flat to show through her prison garb. She'd lost her husband to a younger, prettier woman, but she didn't look as if she'd liked having him around all that much to begin with. She didn't

25

look as if she'd made him like being around her either.

Her dark leaden eyes stared at me when I entered the cubicle. She didn't respond when I introduced myself; she only looked unblinkingly. She'd have showed more animation if they'd wheeled in her dinner tray.

The female guard turned a key in the door and went down another hall, leaving us alone. Carla waited, giving me the expectant kind of look she'd give a calendar. I told her again what my name was, in case she hadn't heard. 'Simon Kaye,' I said. 'Private detective.' Then I said that Leonard Wood thought I might be able to help her. Finally I told her that Leonard Wood was a lawyer—her lawyer.

That got a response. She called him a dirty name and spat on the floor. She was a charmer, that one. I couldn't blame Matt Brent for swapping her for a sexy doll. I'd have swapped her for a pail and mop.

However, there was no point in getting riled. She wasn't *my* wife.

The sweetness and light approach hadn't worked, so I changed weapons. 'What's wrong with you,' I snapped. 'You think everybody's your enemy? What do you think I'm doing here? Why do you think I've come?'

'I don't know,' she muttered, lowering her

eyes. At least she'd stopped challenging me.

'Give a guess!'

She looked away, and the corner of her thin-lipped mouth tightened. 'Because Mr Wood told you to come.'

'That's good. That's very good. And the reason is that he wants to help you out of the spot you're in. He's on your side, and I'm on your side. Does that get through to you?'

She sneered and called him another name. This time she didn't spit.

I got sharp with her again. 'What's he done to make you dislike him? What's with you anyway? Is it that you don't like his looks?'

She gave me a scathing glare. 'He wants me to plead guilty.'

'To murder?'

'That's right.'

'I think you misunderstand. He wants you to plead guilty to manslaughter. There's a big difference.'

'I don't know what the difference is. All I know is he wants me to say I killed that sonuvabitch husband of mine over another woman. I'd kill him over a lot of things, but not over another woman. She could have him.'

'You're saying it *wasn't* over this other woman?'

'That's right,' she snapped. 'I never even

heard of her. I didn't know there was such a thing. I don't know who'd have him.'

'So what *did* you kill him for?'

She stopped and looked at me. 'Now you're sounding just like my goddamn lawyer, you sonuvabitch. You're trying to trick me into saying I killed him.'

'Well, didn't you?'

'Of course not! What the hell would I kill the bastard for? He was my meal ticket. You think I'm dumb or something?'

'That's the only reason you wanted him around?'

'Give me another reason. If you knew the bastard, you wouldn't even ask such a question.'

I said, 'I see.' There was fire in her eyes and dark thoughts behind. Matt Brent had lived with a keg of gun powder. I went on slowly. 'Then, if you needed him as a meal ticket, and another woman took him away...'

She called me one of the names she reserved for Leonard Wood. 'You're just like him,' she snarled. 'You talk just the way he does. If I'm gonna lose my meal ticket anyway, I might as well kill him. That's what you're thinking, isn't it?'

'Let's say the possibility occurs to me.'

'Except that if he ditched me, I could get alimony.'

'And if you killed him, you could get his insurance...maybe.'

She glared at me. 'Get the hell out of here. You're no more good to me than my bastard lawyer.'

'Sorry,' I said and held up a hand. 'I'm putting words in your mouth. What's *your* story?'

She fixed me with knifelike eyes. 'I didn't know he had a damned mistress. That's the first thing. The second is, I couldn't've cared less. He could screw every skirt in town for all of me. So I'm not going to have Wood or anybody else trying to make me say I killed him for that.'

'Go on.'

'The next point is, I didn't kill him at all. That's another piece of crap I'm not going to put up with.' She leaned forward and said through her teeth, 'Didn't I just finish telling you he was my meal ticket and I wanted him healthy?'

I said, very seriously, 'I see. You're saying you didn't kill him at all, because you needed him as a meal ticket?'

'That's right.' She sat back. 'At least you're showing more sense than that Wood bastard.'

'Well, what did happen then? Who *did* kill him?'

29

'I don't know who it was. I never saw him before.'

It was going to be like that, eh? I said, 'Someone else came in and committed the crime? That's what you're saying?'

She smote herself on the forehead. 'Comes the light! Don't tell me I've found somebody who understands English!'

'You've told this to Wood?'

'That's right. And to everybody else. But nobody understands English. Only you. Only *you* seem to get the idea.' She grabbed and shook my hand. 'Congratulations.'

So she'd been telling her tale of innocence hither and yon, and nobody had believed her. Now she was going to try it on me. I could hardly wait. 'Well, well,' I said heartily, 'now you've got a listener. Let's hear your story.'

She had a listener and I had a friend. Her eyes were warm now, meltingly warm, her face alive. It was a dark, swarthy face, a lean face, and there were the beginning threads of grey in her hair. 'I suppose we were in love once, Matt and me,' she started.

'Hold it.'

She paused. 'I want to tell you what happened.'

'I want to know what happened *that* night.'

'Yes, but you won't understand about that

night unless—'

'I don't have to understand,' I said. 'Understanding can come later. What I need to know now is what you believe—'

She jerked upright. 'I *believe?*' Her eyes were ice cubes again. 'You're like the others! You think I'm making it up!'

She was one touchy bitch. Maybe I shouldn't blame her. I wasn't in her spot. I placated her. 'Sorry about that. I'm talking about what happened, and you should do the talking. What did *you* see and experience?'

Either I mollified her or she needed a listener. She went on. 'First of all,' she said, 'my husband was out. I was in the front room watching television. I had it up pretty loud, of course. Then it was around half-past ten and Matt came in—'

'Know where he'd been?'

'No. What would I care?'

'You wouldn't know whether he'd been with that woman or not?'

She said harshly, 'I just told you I didn't give a damn where he went or what he did or who he did it with. Are you gonna let me tell my story?'

'Continue.'

'So it's about half-past ten and Matt comes home and he goes into the bedroom and the

31

next thing I know, I hear a shot. You get me? I hear a shot—a gun going off.

'Well, I jump up and I run for the bedroom. I don't know what's happened, whether Matt was trying to commit suicide or there was a burglar in there or what. So I'm running to the bedroom calling, "Matt!" and there's this masked man in there with a gun, and Matt's on the bed, bleeding, and this man with the mask grabs me as soon as I come in and shoves me in a corner and tells me not to move. And then he shoots Matt five more times while he's lying there, and when he's all through, he grabs me again and sticks the gun in my hand and gives me a shove toward the bed, and he ducks out and leaves me there.'

That's where she stopped. Now she watched me, hawk-eyed, to see how well her story went over.

You make up stories like that in kindergarten, but I played it deadpan. I said to her, 'What did the man look like?'

'I told you, he was wearing a mask.'

'What kind of a mask?'

'A ski mask. Like burglars wear.'

'You mean like *robbers* wear?'

'What's the difference?'

'Burglars try to steal where nobody'll see them. They're not as likely to wear masks.'

'This one had a mask,' she answered belligerently.

So, he had a mask? 'What colour hair?'

'He was wearing a hat.'

'What kind of a hat?'

'I don't know. Some kind of a cap thing.'

'Colour?'

'Dark...brown or black or something. What difference does it make? I don't know what he looked like.'

'What about his clothes?'

'Dark.'

'Jacket?'

'I didn't notice. I think so.'

'Is there anything about him that stood out in particular? Was there some quirk or a loose thread or an untied shoelace?'

She shook her head and bitched about questions like that. I expected she would.

'Was he wearing gloves? Think carefully now. You saw he was holding a gun. Could you see his hands?'

Her mouth twitched. 'I don't know.'

She wasn't going to be pinned down one bit. I gave it one further try. 'Was he right- or left-handed?'

'Right,' she said without hesitation.

'You don't have any trouble remembering that, then?'

'I was on that side. I saw the gun. Besides, that's what the cops and that Mr Wood asked me.'

'And the gun he gave you—the one he shot your husband with—was that *his* gun?'

'It was Matt's gun.'

I took a couple of heavy breaths. Carla had worked hard figuring out the answers to all the wrong things. She should have known that the mysterious stranger alibi is the oldest one in the books. If Leonard Wood could not get her to listen to reason, she'd be in the soup. He'd be trying to get her off on manslaughter and she'd be trying to plead not guilty.

It wasn't my business, and I can't say I ached for her. (I wanted to see her get it if you want to know.) But I had to take a crack at showing her how futile her alibi was. I said, trying to sound like a reporter gathering news. 'This masked burglar who was in your bedroom, how did he get into the house?'

Her answer was quick. 'Through the back door, I expect. It wasn't locked.'

'He would have had a gun of his own, of course?'

'I don't know. If he did, I didn't see it.'

'It would be a little difficult to imagine his taking your husband's gun away from him otherwise.'

She didn't change her story. 'I didn't see any other gun. He probably caught my husband by surprise.'

'Even so, it would be difficult for him to disarm your husband unless he had a weapon of his own, wouldn't you say?'

'I didn't see any other gun,' she repeated.

'You believe your husband entered the bedroom and the burglar caught him by surprise?'

'That's right.'

'Except that if you had the TV playing pretty loud, it would be more likely that your husband would catch the burglar by surprise.'

Her eyes darkened. 'I don't care what you say,' she answered. 'I'm telling you what happened.'

'And the burglar shoots your husband once? And when you come into the room, he makes you watch while he shoots your husband five more times?'

'That's right.'

'Do you have any idea why he killed your husband?'

She shrugged. 'I don't know. Maybe he thought Matt could identify him.'

'With a ski mask on?'

When trapped, she turned vicious. 'Well, how the hell should I know why he shot him?'

'And he didn't shoot him just once, he shot

35

him six times? It doesn't take six bullets to kill a man.'

'Maybe he was excited.'

'He kills your husband, presumably to eliminate a witness. But he didn't try to kill you? You were a witness, too.'

'Maybe he figured the cops'd decide I did it and he'd get rid of me that way.'

She seemed to think that was logical, which told me I was getting nowhere. I gave it one last try. 'And the burglar, after killing your husband, shoved the gun into your hand and ran away? Is that right?'

'That's exactly right.'

'Back or front door?'

She wouldn't fall for it. 'I don't know. I was standing in the bedroom. You can damned well believe I was in shock. I didn't know what else was going on.'

Last call. 'What'd he take with him?'

'With him?'

'He was a burglar, you say. Your husband caught him in the act of burgling in your bedroom. Presumably the room had been ransacked...drawers open, things like that. The burglar *did* steal something, didn't he?'

She shook her head, her mouth a thin line.

'Nothing had been touched? Nothing had been taken? The burglar just killed your husband and left?'

'Stop trying to make it sound so funny,' she snapped. 'He probably hadn't had time to do anything.'

'I see. Then what happened?'

'One of the neighbours came over and I told him somebody shot Matt. Then the police came.'

'When did you find out your husband had been seeing another woman?'

'That's just hearsay. Personally, I don't believe it.'

That tore it. I stood up. 'You know, you're hurting yourself with that attitude. You aren't hurting anybody but yourself. If you're smart, you'll face up to a few things.'

She moved closer. 'Listen, if you think you're going to make me say I killed Matt, forget it.'

'Somebody did.' I gave her a last chance. 'Did your husband have any enemies?'

'Not that I know of, but I can't say he had any friends either.'

'Nobody had threatened him? He never acted nervous or uneasy?'

That time she bit. Her eyes widened. 'Yeah, I see what you mean. Maybe it wasn't a burglar after all. Maybe somebody was out to get Matt. Maybe he arrested somebody, or broke up a drug ring,' she said, reflectively. 'Now that you mention it, I think maybe he *was* a little nervous of late.'

The bitch would try *anything* in the hope that something would work. I said, with a certain glee. 'Except he was executive secretary to the chief of police. He didn't go out in the field.'

I won't tell you the names she called me. The essence was that, like everyone else, I wanted to railroad her too.

CHAPTER FOUR

'You've got yourself a pip,' I told Leonard Wood back in the waiting room. 'I don't know how you're going to get her to accept manslaughter. She doesn't live in the real world.'

He gave me a spectral smile. 'I tried to have a psychiatrist examine her. She threw him out.'

'That's because he's part of the real world. So's a manslaughter plea. She'd rather pretend it was spies and secret enemies and a Mata Hari go-go dancer whom she never knew existed.'

Leonard Wood's smile turned to a grimace. 'That's another of my problems. She's known about Nerissa Claire all along.'

We were walking out into the mid-afternoon sunshine, and I stopped on the steps. 'She knows? And she pretends she doesn't know?'

'Let's put it this way. The neighbours heard Matt and Carla fight about Nerissa Claire a dozen times. More than that, she created a disturbance at Frank's Bar one night when Nerissa was performing.'

'You're kidding!'

He shook his head. '*I'm* not kidding. Maybe Ben Schill is kidding. He manages Frank's Bar. Maybe the other witnesses are kidding...or they're identifying the wrong woman. But *I'm* not kidding.'

I could feel sorry for the guy. Carla Brent was a disaster area. He didn't want her case any more than I did, but he had no choice.

He walked me to my heap—his limousine stood half the lot away—and I said to him. 'Knowing how Carla feels, do you still want me to track down the Claire girl?'

He nodded. 'I'll need her sometime before this is over. Carla will have to listen to reason eventually. It's a matter of getting her to understand.'

'I don't envy you your job.'

'I don't know that I envy you yours. What're you going to do now?'

I said that Frank's Bar was the next priority.

Frank's Bar is in the downtown section, on LaVerne Street, as Leonard Wood had mentioned, but out where LaVerne gets flaky, where the massage parlours and porno shops sprout, where 'topless' is part of the message and 'bottomless' lies around a still seamier corner.

There were picture panels in the frame around the door. The girls in the pictures were featured full-length, shapely and scantily clad, but revealing less than you'll see any day on the beach. The faces of the girls, coyly cocked at the camera, had the same monotonous prettiness that made only their hairstyles distinctive. The photos were tinted, faded, and bore no names. The girls could have been mothers of the present performers.

The neon sign above the outer door didn't say, Frank's Bar, it said, Frank's Topless Bar, the word Topless blinking. Inside the inner door was a dim, tight room with the bar down one wall and as many tables and chairs to the right of the barstools as could fit on the rest of the property. The stage on which the girls performed was a four-foot square platform flush with the bar top, enclosed on three sides by black plywood so that only the customers could see the acts. There was a baby spot overhead and a few wisps of black velvet for decor. Access was up steps from a narrow passage behind the bar.

Outside, it was hot and bright, not quite three o'clock in the afternoon. Inside, the windows had been painted over, and it was hot and dull, with the air of a fetid summer night. Half a dozen customers lined the bar and watched TV. The platform was empty and the baby spot was out.

The bartender came my way. He looked like the bouncer. I said I wanted to talk to Ben Schill. He said, 'What for?' I said, 'What do I need, your permission?'

He looked at me through squinty eyes, and a couple of customers held their breath. He was shorter than I by half a head but he had a Tony Galento physique. He could have thrown the bar at me. He didn't. He went away and came back.

Then a king-sized edition of the bartender appeared at my shoulder. He was three inches taller than I and a hundred pounds heavier. He had a large, thin nose, big white teeth, the grin of a hungry shark, and a smelly cigar. He stood a little too close, looked down and said, 'I'm Ben Schill.'

I said I was pleased to meet him, my name

41

was Simon Kaye and I was a private investigator. I gave him my card and he held it close, trying to read it. Then the baby spot went on, and mounting the steps to the top of the bar was an attractive young brunette wearing black, skin-tight pants under a skirt of ankle-length strings of beads, and on top, a diaphanous hip-length cape with silver trim, held together by a silver clip at her throat.

There was applause from the customers, and she beamed a smile at the wall over their heads, unfastened the clip and revealed a pair of very full, very well-shaped breasts. She hung the cape on an invisible hook and started slowly to gyrate. There was a brief accompaniment of wolf whistles, and the bartender switched off the TV.

Ben Schill paid no attention to the girl. He moved closer to the spot the better to read my card. The girl looked down at him and at me and watched us while she twisted and turned.

Ben turned to me, his eyes hooded. 'What's this about? Nerissa Claire?'

My nod perked up his grin. 'Come to my office,' he said in greasy welcome-mat tones and looked for the first time at the girl. She looked at him, he made a snapping sound with my card and she responded by repasting her smile in place and doubling her pace, shimmy-

ing and shaking and making her breasts
bounce. He led me away, zig-zagging among
the empty tables to a door at the back and
I, with a final glance at the girl, followed.
She was watching us go and her smile said,
'Drop dead.'

'She gets paid to run, not walk,' Ben Schill
confided as he brought me into a small clut-
tered office with shelves, a desk, a number of
chairs, a dirty-window view of the alley and a
mess of papers and ledgers.

'A lot of paper work,' he said with a wave
and sat behind his desk. He studied my card
again, rubbing his thumb over the printing.
'Nerissa Claire, huh? I figured that.' He grinned up at me. 'I guess you can say I'm something of a detective too.'

I sat in a wooden armchair. 'She quit two
weeks ago tonight, I understand?'

'Yeah. You think you can find her?'

'With a little help from people like you.'

He sat forward and spoke to me in low,
super-sincere tones. 'Well, when you do, it's
worth a fifty to me if you'll let me know. It's
important that I see her. I got a very important message for her. Very important.'

'I'll make note of that,' I said, just as sin-
cerely, and wrote it down in my little black
book. 'Phone number?'

43

He read it off the phone beside him and sat back to puff his cigar. 'How long d'ya think it'll take?'

'It depends on what I can find out.'

'I'll give you everything I've got,' Schill said. He opened a bottom desk drawer, examined some folders and handed one to me. It was Nerissa Claire's and contained her job application, her pay sheet, address and phone number, and her work schedule. The application was dated the previous October, listed her age as twenty-four; height: five-feet-four; weight: one hundred and five; dimensions: thirty-five, twenty-two, thirty-six; hair: brown; eyes: brown; no visible scars. The rest of the items on the sheet—education, previous employment, next of kin and place of birth— were blank.

Ben Schill, an elbow on his chair arm, picking his teeth with my card, was leaning back watching me craftily. I said, 'Too bad you didn't make her fill out the rest of her application.'

'Sorry about that,' he answered. 'Never thought it'd matter.'

I picked up her work sheet. It scheduled her for the three to eleven p.m. shift every third week, and five p.m. to one a.m. the other two, six days a week. Pay was a little over the mini-

44

wage but not enough to cause a stampede. Ben Schill, when he saw me get to that, pointed his cigar at the sheet and said, 'That doesn't include tips.'

'Tips?'

'Well, a percentage. They sit with the customers between times. You know, put on a slinky dress and rub knees. The customers buy them drinks. Of course, it's only tea. Can't have the girls getting smashed. And they get a percentage of the drink tab.'

'In other words, they make more money wearing a dress than not wearing a dress?'

'You mean sitting instead of dancing?' He grinned. 'Yeah, that's true. But you have to realize it's *not* wearing the dress that gets the customers in here in the first place.'

'Forty-eight hours a week? No overtime?'

'Can't afford it,' Schill said with a shake of his head. 'Can only budget so much. The girls prefer it that way. Hire a fourth girl and they'd have to split the dough four ways. After Nerissa left, Dana—' he waved his cigar at the door, '—that's the one who's out there now...she and Lucille wanted to do it all, the two of them. But that's too big a load. It takes three girls to handle it right. Believe me, I've been around the business long enough to know. And they got no kick.' He waved the cigar some more.

'They make two hundred and fifty a week, maybe more, plus anything they can pick up on the outside. That's not bad for unskilled labour. I mean, any moron can wiggle her hips.'

From the clientele in the place, all those girls could pick up on the outside would be a salami sandwich, but Ben Schill didn't seem to be hurting. One of his performers had quit two weeks ago, and he hadn't had trouble replacing her.

I said, 'She came to work for you last October? How do you hire these girls?'

'Simple. I bring 'em in here, tell 'em to strip and do a dance for me. If they're hesitant or unwilling, or if they don't have a good pair of tits, the hell with 'em. If the broad looks okay, I call in the help—Jerry behind the bar, the kid who sweeps up, a couple of the chefs from next door—and have them look her over. If she balks at showing off everything she's got to them, then she's in the wrong business.'

'Everything?'

'That's right. We aren't a bottomless bar yet, but maybe one of these days we'll get to be, and I don't want the girls going chicken on me. Besides, if she doesn't like showing off what's downstairs, she's not going to be happy showing off what's upstairs, and a go-go dancer, to be good, has got to be proud of herself. She's got to like what she's got and like to show it off.'

'So Nerissa came in here and put on a show for you and you hired her?'

'Yeah.' Ben Schill smiled at the memory. 'And I don't mind telling you, she was a cutie.'

'Do they have to do more than show off for you to get the job? Are there, shall we say "extras" involved?'

'Oh, hell no. I don't run that kind of a place. This is strictly legit. The guys around here... work for me...they treat the girls like their sisters. We're very protective about those girls.'

'So if one of the girls starts to go out with a customer, there's no jealousy or anything?'

Schill laughed. 'You're talking about Nerissa and that cop she went with?' He sobered abruptly. 'You think anybody here's gonna try to interfere with a cop? If a cop wants to take out one of the girls, you let him take her out. I don't need getting on the bad side of cops.'

'What if he hadn't been a cop?'

Schill shook his head and assured me it wouldn't have made any difference. 'Nerissa led her own life on her own time,' he told me. 'All the girls do. She got herself involved in

47

a tragedy, but it wasn't her fault.'

'She quit the night of the tragedy. Was it because Matt Brent had been killed?'

Schill frowned. 'I don't know what was bugging her that night. She just told me she wanted her pay right through that night, that she was leaving.'

'No notice, no warning, no reason?'

'That's right. I couldn't figure it out. Then, when I heard about the shooting, I thought that might've had something to do with it, but I don't know how she found out.'

'The police didn't come to see her?'

'Not till the next day.'

I asked him to give it to me in detail and he stopped picking his teeth long enough to tell me the story. Around ten-thirty that evening, he said, she came to his office. She was dressed, meaning she'd been sitting with customers, and she told him she'd be quitting when she finished at eleven that night. She wasn't coming back and she wanted her pay. She wouldn't give a reason and she seemed mad about something. She was still supposed to dance again, and she insisted on getting her pay or she'd stand up the customers.

Schill gave her the money and went with her to the dressing room while she got ready for the final dance, but she wouldn't explain anything. She was adamant that this was her last performance, and when she was through her act, she returned to the dressing room to put on her clothes and ignored all Schill's pleas and questions. She walked out of the bar at quarter-past eleven and that was the last he'd seen of her.

I mulled that one over and checked Nerissa's work sheet. Schill hadn't mistaken the time. Nerissa was on the three-to-eleven shift that week. Matt Brent had been killed about ten-thirty on the other side of town and at about the same time Nerissa told Ben Schill she was quitting. There was no way she could have known he was dead when she gave Schill her notice.

That raised the question: would she have given her notice if she *had* known?

I said, 'Was Matt Brent here earlier that evening?'

Schill couldn't say. 'But I wouldn't be surprised. He was here most nights, part of the evening at least.

'I got a theory about this case,' he added. 'I think she and the cop were going to run off together. But when he went home to get his things, his wife found out and put a stop to it.' He looked at me expectantly. 'What do you think?'

'It's a possibility.'

'His wife came in and raised hell here one night, you know.'

'I'd like to hear about that.'

'She got the wrong girl. Matt was sitting with Dana Doxey. Nerissa was dancing and Dana was waiting her turn. So in comes this woman and tries to jump all over Dana, calling her Nerissa, and when Matt stops her, she tries to claw his eyes out. Matt got her out of there, carted her off—home, I guess.'

'She was his wife?'

'We don't know it for a fact, but that's what we figure.'

'What'd she look like?'

Ben Schill shrugged. 'Tallish, I guess. Darkish. She had a coat on.'

'Would you recognize her if you saw her again?'

He shook his head. 'It's dark in the bar. And it was all over in a minute. Matt had her out of there in two shakes. But that's the kind of woman who'd shoot up a man. She wouldn't let him run off with Nerissa.'

'So where's Nerissa? Did she run off by herself?'

'I don't know what she did with herself,' Schill confessed with obvious bewilderment. 'I checked around. I thought she might be go-

go dancing at one of the other bars—you know, when her plans fell through. Like I say, I'm kind of a detective myself.' He shook his head. 'But it's not around town. It might be some other city, though. You'll probably find her dancing in some other bar.'

'Did she have a problem with people who work here, or with some of the customers?'

He laughed harshly. 'Like I told you, her going with a cop? There ain't nobody going to hassle her one bit.'

I gave him back his folder and thanked him and asked if I could talk to Dana, the go-go dancer presently performing.

He rose with me. 'Sure. I'll introduce you.' When he opened the door, he said, 'Now you got to admit I'm co-operating. But, like I say, I want to find her too. I've got an important message for her.'

'What's the message?'

'Never mind. It's personal.'

CHAPTER FIVE

In the bar proper the baby spot was out and the go-go girl was gone. All that remained was the empty black box she'd danced in. Ben Schill led me across the back of the long room to a locked door opposite his, beside the lavatories. He gave it two sharp raps and it was opened by the girl named Dana Doxey, who peeked around the edge. Schill didn't wait for her to pull the door wide in invitation; he pushed it from her grip and shoved his bulk through the narrow opening, leaving me to follow.

The room was tiny, with a couch, chair and vanity, and barely room to move between. Just past the end of the couch was the entrance to the cramped corridor that led behind the bar shelves to the dancing platform.

With three of us in the room, it was hard to turn around. Dana was holding a nail file and was dressed in her beaded skirt and diaphanous cape. She looked from one to the other of us, waiting to learn our business.

'Hey, Dana,' Schill boomed, his voice resonant in the closet-like room. 'This here's Simon Kaye, a private detective. He's looking for Nerissa. He wants to ask you some questions.'

He squeezed out past me and shut the door, leaving us alone, Dana shrugged tired shoulders and looked at her watch. Since her cape was only fastened at the throat, the actions of her hands spread it open down the front. Not that she cared. In fact, since the cape was see-through, it didn't matter anyway.

'I got six minutes,' she told me. 'Then I go back on. Fifteen minutes on stage, ten minutes off. You get the idea?'

I said six minutes wouldn't be a very long time.

She sat down in front of the vanity and looked at me in the mirror, smoothing on lipstick with a finger. 'Well, you can wait for me,' she said.

I let myself down on the couch. 'Fifteen minutes is a long time to wait for a ten-minute break.'

'You're telling me.' She started filing bright red nails. 'Well, you've now got five minutes. That ought to be enough to talk about Nerissa, unless that's only a gag and Ben brought you here for something else.'

'You think he might have...brought me here

for something else?'

'He might give it a try. He's done it with the others. But not this time of day. Not when there's only one of us performing.'

'You let him get away with it?'

'He hasn't tried it with me.'

'But the others?'

'Yeah, but I don't know the arrangements.' She gestured at the mirror with her nail file. 'That couch isn't just for sitting on, you know.'

'Ten minutes isn't much time.'

'The Ben Schill types don't need much time. They never heard of foreplay.'

'Was Nerissa one of those who had arrangements?'

'Her?' Dana laughed. 'She'd've had to do it in the john. That cop boyfriend she had watched her like a hawk. I wouldn't've wanted to get caught by him fooling around with Nerissa. If I was Nerissa, I wouldn't want to get caught either.'

'Ben Schill wants to know where Nerissa went. He says he has a message for her. Know what it would be?'

'Sure, that he'll break both her legs if she doesn't come back to work for him again. Business is way off the last couple of weeks.'

She rose, turned sideways to the mirror and slid her hands down over her smooth flat abdomen, analysing herself critically. 'Well,' she said. 'It's time to go give the men something to get excited about again. You going to wait around?'

The room was stifling and shabby. It smelled of powder and perfume, like milady's boudoir after she's gone to Europe—there was the same stale, empty quality. Even with a half-naked Dana posing in front of the mirror, the room was still empty.

I stood up beside her. 'When do you eat?'

'When I get home tonight.'

'There's no supper break or anything?'

'Are you kidding?'

'All right, how about letting me take you out for a bite when you get through? Then we'll have a chance to talk.'

She shook her head. 'No go. You want to talk, wait here.'

'What's wrong with later?'

'Guys take girls out to dinner for only one reason, and I'm not that hungry.'

'No passes. I promise.' I looked her over. 'Not to say that you aren't tempting. But it's strictly business. I really want to talk.'

She checked her makeup one last time. 'That's supposed to make everything all right. It's all business, you say, and I'm supposed to believe you because you stand this close without touching me.'

'Enormous self-control,' I said. 'What if I only buy you ham and eggs? That shouldn't entitle me to do more than hold your hand.'

She looked at me musingly in the mirror. 'I'll think about it,' she said.

'What time do you get through?'

'Eleven. If you come early, you can buy me a drink.'

'Uh-uh,' I said. 'I don't like being taken any more than you do.'

I stopped by police headquarters after Dana Doxey went into her dance. I wanted the department's response to Matt Brent's murder. Al Conflex was the duty sergeant and a friend from way back. He said, 'You must've known Matt. He was in your time. Of course he wasn't very sociable, kind of hard to know. Well, it's a blow having a friend get killed, even so. But it's not like it was line of duty. And he wasn't all that popular. He wasn't popular with the public either—hard to get along with. I think that's why he got reassigned to the chief's office—personal secretary. Plus he had the skills, of course.' He shrugged. 'I'm not knocking the guy. I mean, we all showed up at the funeral. But we'll manage to get along without him, if you know what I mean.'

I said I knew what he meant, and who was in charge of the case? That was Detective Sergeant Dan Saxton, Al told me, but Dan was tied up masterminding a raid on a garage suspected of being headquarters of a stolen-car ring. 'You know about the stolen-car ring, don't you?' he said.

'Only what I've read in the papers.'

'It's big, Simon. Cars disappearing all over the city, and we don't know where they go. The mayor and the aldermen are riding our tails. You won't get near Dan Saxton before the weekend, and if this raid is another fiasco, you're not going to see him then. He's not sweating, he's bleeding.'

That wasn't going to do me much good so I said, 'Who else was in on the Brent case?'

Conflex checked the log and looked at the clock. It was five after four. 'You're in luck,' he said. 'Guy just come off duty—Dennis O'Malley. He was the first officer on the scene. Nice kid. In fact, he was Brent's partner till Brent became the chief's secretary. You want to talk to him?'

'If he'll talk to me.'

We went to the locker room, where remnants of the four o'clock shift were still on tap. O'Malley was grooming himself for a date, running a comb again and again through lush dark locks.

Conflex introduced me, telling O'Malley I was a pariah, a cop who'd gone civilian, but I just might not sell out my grandmother. So if he wanted to answer my questions, he, Sergeant Conflex, wouldn't take offence.

O'Malley was eager to get to his waiting lady and now I was dumped on him and he smiled at me like I was castor oil. When I found he didn't have a car and offered him a ride, his smile became real.

We went crosstown and O'Malley turned downright chatty. Sure he knew Matt Brent. They'd been partners when O'Malley first made patrolman. He knew Carla too, but not well. She wasn't the kind of person anyone got to know well.

I mentioned Carla's mysterious stranger alibi, and he made a face. 'You'd think a cop's wife would know better than to pull a fairy tale like that,' he said. 'If she knew anything about the police department she'd know that one wouldn't go.'

'How much *did* she know about the department? Did she come around? Did she socialize with the other wives?'

O'Malley didn't think so. The only contact he ever had with her was going to their house to ride to work with Matt. 'I don't have a car,' he explained. 'I'm saving my dough.'

'Was there much hostility between them?'

'Not when I knew them, back three to four years ago. I don't mean they acted like love-birds. It was just kinda live-and-let-live.' He sighed at the tragedy. 'Believe me,' he said, 'when my sweetie and I get hitched, we're never going to stop holding hands. You married, Mr Kaye?'

'Not so far.'

'I'm all for it. You got a girl you really love and you got the privilege of sharing a home with her, building a life together... There's nothing like it. That's why I can't see why Matt and Carla got hitched. If you aren't crazy about each other, what's the point?'

'Good luck, sweet prince.'

'What?'

'Don't mind me. I'm cynical. I haven't found that kind of a girl yet. And, to tell the truth, I don't expect to. So, you're lucky, and Matt wasn't lucky. Speaking of that, why do you think Carla killed him?'

'If you want to know, I think she found out he was going to leave her. Of course that's not what *she* says.'

'What does she say, besides blaming the murder on a mysterious stranger?'

'She swore up and down she never knew

there was another woman,' he said sadly. 'And here you've got the neighbours testifying she and Matt used to have knockdown drag-out fights over her. They say you could hear Carla a block away.'

I asked for a rundown on the night in question, and he said the first word the police got was when John Oates, a neighbour, called in that there'd been a shooting next door and Matt Brent was dead.

'I was in a cruiser when it came through and it hit me kinda hard, Matt having been my partner. Not that I'd seen much of him after he got reassigned as the chief's secretary. I mean, he was in on all the inside stuff that's only for the top brass and I'm only a lowly patrolman, so our paths didn't cross. And, of course, he was on the day shift all the time and wasn't rotating like the rest of us.' O'Malley relaxed against the corner of the door and regarded me levelly. He was a tall, lanky Irishman, handsome as hell, with chalk-white skin and still-soft eyes. They'd harden in time. Few eyes harden more than a cop's. Few other eyes see so much.

'You were first on the scene?' I said.

'Yes. The first.' He looked out at the road reflectively. 'Oates was waiting for us—for my partner and me. The story he gave us was that he heard all this shooting next door and ran over to see what was going on. Carla met him at the door, he said, holding Matt's revolver in her hand, and she told him that somebody'd shot her husband. Oates wanted to help and tried to enter, but she wouldn't let him. She said Matt was dead and he couldn't come in. So he went back and phoned emergency.'

'Then what?'

'I rang Carla's bell and she answered.'

'Still holding the gun?'

'Not now.'

'How was she? Was she in shock?'

He shook his head. 'The best I can describe it, she could've been letting me in to ride to work with Matt, the way she used to. She opened the door and saw me standing there, and before I could even say, "Hello, Carla," she nodded at the bedroom and said, "He's in there." '

I stopped at a light and looked at O'Malley. He was watching the street as a good cop should. 'So,' he continued slowly, 'I went in, and he was there all right. He was on the bed with holes all over him, but the blood had stopped leaking out. He was just a corpse.'

'What about the gun?'

'It was on the bed beside the body. Carla must have chucked it there after she saw

Oates. Anyway, she was at my shoulder and I said, "Did you do this?" and she said, "Do you think I'm crazy?" or something like that. So I said, "Who did it then?" and she said, "A burglar." '

He snorted and I snorted and moved when the light changed. I said, 'That neighbour, Oates. Do you know anything about his story?'

'I was there when Sergeant Saxton questioned him, if that's what you mean.'

'How did he describe the shots? Did they come all at once, six in a row?'

O'Malley nodded solemnly. 'You're thinking about Carla's story—that there was a first shot and she ran to the bedroom, then the mysterious stranger fired five more shots.' He shrugged and said, 'Turn right at the next corner. It's the third house on the right. Well, Mr Kaye, I guess you know what witnesses are worth when it comes to what they see and hear. There were a lot of conflicting stories about those shots. First, according to Mr Oates, they all came at once. Six shots, one after the other.

'As for his wife, she thinks they were spasmodic—a couple, a pause, another one or two, another pause, then the rest.'

'Any of the other neighbours hear anything?'

O'Malley nodded. 'Oh, yes. They all heard shots. A mile away, people were hearing shots.

But with them it's not a question of how they were spaced, it's a question of how many. Some think they heard three shots; there are others who swear they heard ten. And there's one couple up the road who claim it was a machine gun.'

I laughed. We both laughed. It meant that the defence counsel had no prayer of convincing a jury that a mysterious stranger had killed Matt. Which, of course, was why Leonard Wood wanted to find the *femme fatale*. Carla, poor dumb Carla, might believe an innocent plea would set her free. The rest of us had a more realistic view. It was enough to make you wonder where she'd been all those years she'd been married to Matt.

That, however, wasn't my concern. My job was to find out where Nerissa Claire had gone. So far, I hadn't latched onto any right tracks.

I let O'Malley off in front of his girl friend's house. It was in the cheek-by-jowl section of town: lower middle-class, one-family dwellings separated by the width of a driveway, fronted by sidewalks and enough lawn to lure sparrows. You didn't really need more to cut the grass than nail scissors, but three property owners on the street were cropping their lawns with power mowers (two swipes, and back to the garage).

One mower-operator was father-of-the-bride-to-be, a plump, grey-haired elf whose mower handles came up to his chin, and O'Malley dragged me out of the car to meet him. Then the girl of his dreams and her mother appeared, and I met them, too. The girl's name was Sharon O'Leary, and she was petite. She came to O'Malley's shoulder when she stood on tiptoe. She had a plain but pleasant face, a small-breasted but adequate figure, her hair was dirty blond, and she'd weigh a hundred pounds if she wore chain mail.

They stood together, and she hung on his arm in the most beautiful way. She said hello to me, but she only saw him. The bunch of us talked for five minutes, mostly about the weather, but the two of them stood in an enchanted circle. The rest of us—the whole of the world—were nothing but backdrop.

It was pretty to see. It was touching, it was sad. It would almost make you believe in True Love.

CHAPTER SIX

It was just after five when I got back to the office, and Eileen was putting the typewriter to bed. She briefed me on messages, and I had her phone Miss Shelly Polk for an interview while I signed letters and cleaned up my desk. Miss Polk was the cousin of Nerissa Claire, who, according to Leonard Wood, had come to the big city to go to modelling school and share Nerissa's condominium. She was, obviously, the next subject on my list.

Eileen came into my office wearing a bemused smile. 'Miss Shelly Polk is on the line,' she said, 'and doesn't seem interested in talking with private detectives. I think you'll have to charm her.'

'You tell her what it was about?' I pressed the connecting button and lifted the phone.

Eileen nodded. 'I said it had to do with Nerissa Claire.'

I spoke into the phone, got no response, and spoke again. Nobody was there. 'Flown the coop,' I said, putting it down. 'What did she sound like?'

Eileen wrinkled her nose. Despite her penchant for low-cut dresses and attracting wolf whistles, she's a modest lass and takes a dim—and perhaps jealous—view of other members of her sex who are, for the most part, much less moderate in their behaviour. 'Very young,' she said. 'Probably below the legal limit.'

By that, she meant attractive and available. You have to know her language. I said, 'I meant, what was her attitude?'

'Oh.' Eileen rearranged her thoughts. 'Alarmed, maybe. Upset. Not in favour.'

'Any reason?'

'She didn't give any.'

'Upset...but not hostile? Only negative?'

'I'd say hostile.'

'But cute?'

Eileen's thoughts went back to where they'd been. 'Unless her diapers need changing.'

That painted Eileen's picture. Shelly Polk was modelled along the lines of the *femme fatale* Leonard Wood wanted to find—wanted *me* to find.

The real message I got from the phone call was not that Shelly Polk refused to see me, it was that she was home. I left her address with Eileen as my next port of call and tooled the heap through the oven of June afternoon air.

The temperature had dropped enough so that the street surfaces were no longer soft, and rivulets of tar had stopped puddling at the edges, but you could still bake a cake on my roof.

The Nerissa Claire-Shelly Polk condo rated three and a half stars on the tour guide. It was new, solid, and in an A-one neighbourhood. No way was it the rent for a go-go dancer whose sugar daddy brought home a cop's salary. Either Matt Brent had income sources Carla didn't know about, or Nerissa Claire hadn't needed his dough and had been seeing him for love. From what I'd heard, Brent hadn't been lovable, but there's no telling what will turn a girl on. Time enough to find out about that. The key to today was Shelly Polk. I rang the doorbell and, in response, she undid the chain and pulled the door wide.

I have to say Shelly Polk looked as good as Eileen was afraid she would. She was petite, blond and gorgeous, with a figure her designer jeans and half opened blouse showed to almost too much advantage. And she wasn't under age, either. From the way the jeans fitted and what the blouse showed, she hadn't been wearing diapers for a long time. In fact, if she went in for go-go dancing, she could stampede the rest of the police department.

One look at her told me a lot about the missing Nerissa. From what Shelly had to flaunt and the way she did it, I knew Nerissa had to have everything Shelly had. It was a sure bet Nerissa wouldn't have roomed with anything better than she was. That kind of grief the Nerissas in the world don't want.

But the king-size welcome the wide-open door provided wasn't meant for me. She breathed relief and said, 'At last!' Then she waved at an empty corner of her elegant living room. 'Put it there. I've cleared everything away.'

I made sure I was inside the door before I answered. 'Put what where?'

'The stereo, of course.' She gave me a shaded look. 'Aren't you delivering my stereo?'

I said, 'That comes with the insurance papers you have to sign. I have to ask you questions about that. For instance, this is the Nerissa Claire apartment?'

Her eyes had become as cold as the air conditioning. I was out of the sauna and into the refrigerator, and now she was making me shiver. She said, 'What's all this!'

'Just a little information.' I took out my notebook and ball-point. 'Your name is Shelly Polk, but this apartment is in the name of Nerissa Claire. Is that right?'

She was already back against the wall, wary and uneasy. 'Ye-es.'

'And this stereo is for...whom?'

She worked her hands together. 'Me,' she said. 'Shelly—'

'Where is Nerissa Claire?'

The girl's eyes were wide and muted. It was hard to tell their colour—something between green and brown. 'She left. She left the first of June.'

'Where did she go?'

Shelly shook her head. 'I don't know. She left to get married. Why do you want to know all this?'

'It's the insurance.'

She looked panicked and pressed herself against the wall. I tried to put her at ease. 'Can we sit down?'

She moved obediently to a couch, leaving me a chair half across the room. I thought she might try to con me with sex appeal, play the boy-girl game, but she was too frightened. She sat, knees together, hands placed so, her head bowed forward, neck exposed, as if she were Mary Queen of Scots awaiting the axe. What was she afraid of? I was only delivering a stereo.

'When did Nerissa Claire leave?'

'First of the month.' She was shivering. 'Why?'

I made myself tiresome, writing down the information. Nothing is as inane and relaxing as bureaucracy. 'How long have *you* been here?'

'Since just before she left. I don't understand—'

I wasn't going to let her understand. 'She left here June first, you say? What time?'

'I don't know. I wasn't here.'

'Did she leave a note...say goodbye?'

The proper forms one always has to fill out have countless questions that appear purposeless. Shelly accepted this one woodenly. 'Yes, she left a note. It said she was leaving to get married.'

'Do you have the note?'

'I threw it away. I didn't know—'

'What else did it say?'

'Nothing else.'

'What did it say you should do about her things? What about the rent? Was there some arrangement about the rent? Did she say when she'd be coming back?'

'No, no.' Shelly came alive. 'Nothing like that. Everything is all right. She'd paid the rent.'

'Whom did she marry?'

That scared the girl again. She trembled. 'I don't know. She didn't say.'

'Nerissa is your cousin, I understand. Where does she come from? Where do her folks live?'

Shelly thought for half a moment, then she said, too quickly, 'They're dead.'

'Where *did* they live?'

'Somewhere in Ohio. I don't know where. She left them years ago.' Shelly was speaking very fast now.

'Where do *your* folks live?'

That brought a touch of hysteria to her response. 'What do you want to know for? They're dead too. Everybody's dead!'

'Tell me about Nerissa Claire. What kind of a girl is she?'

'What? Why?'

'She's responsible for this condominium,' I pontificated. 'We have to make sure about such things. Or is someone else responsible?'

'No, no,' Shelly said quickly. 'She's the one responsible. And she's fine. She's good. She's very good. She's a nice girl. You don't have to worry about her.'

'What does she look like?'

'Pretty.'

'As pretty as you?'

'Prettier.' She stopped and frowned. Suspicion was replacing hysteria. 'What's that got to do with it?'

'We have to make sure. What about her hob-

71

bies? Likes and dislikes? Ambitions? Friends? Who were her friends?'

'I don't know. I didn't know her that well.' Shelly was growing alarmed. 'Who are you? What do you want?'

'Whom else did she play around with besides Matt Brent?'

Shelly sat up and the game was over. 'I don't know what you're talking about. I don't know about her friends. You're not from the insurance company!' Her eyes widened in terror. 'Who are you? What do you want?'

There was a knock on the door and she flew to it as to salvation. Standing in the gap was a husky, sweaty male in khaki coveralls, holding an invoice. 'Shelly Polk?' he said. 'This the place? We got a stereo to deliver.'

She clung to the doorknob and nodded. 'Yes, yes.' She gestured at me. 'Who's this man?'

The husky male arched an eyebrow my way. 'I don't know, ma'am. I never saw him before.' He turned back towards the loading truck.

She wheeled on me, shaking and wild. 'Who are you? What are you doing to me?'

I handed her my business card, the one that says I'm a private detective and gives an address and phone.

She read it. 'A detective!' She made it sound worse than 'rapist!' And, of course, recog-

72

nition dawned. 'You're the one...!' She tore the card in two and threw it at me. Then she burst into tears of relief. 'Get out, get out,' she cried. 'Don't ever come near me again!'

There are times when departure is appropriate.

This was one such.

CHAPTER SEVEN

The condo set up that Shelly lived in was like my own—so arranged that the entrances were hidden from one other, thus providing a maximum amount of privacy in a minimum amount of space. It's great for the inhabitants, for even nosy neighbours are hard put to know what you're up to. But it's not very good for detectives on a stake-out.

That was my problem when I left Shelly's pad. She was a fraud and as phony as a sidewalk salesman's diamond rings. I didn't know how much of what she said was a lie, but the smart money bet was to assume a hundred percent and work your way down. And that left the question, 'Why did she lie?' What did she know that Nerissa didn't want told?

The point was, I wouldn't find out by asking. I'd have to do it by tailing. But there was no place where I could watch her door without being in plain view. The best I could do was watch the roadway that led to her door.

It was only six o'clock, the sun was still high, and mine was the only car in the condo complex that was parked on the street. A detective on a stake-out doesn't want to be conspicuous. I made bets with myself as to how long it'd be before some four-year-old kid asked me what I was doing.

More to the point, though, it was still warm out and I was thirsty. In a little while I'd also start getting hungry. I'd passed a fast-food joint half a mile away on the trip over, and the temptation was strong to hop there and bring back a hamburger and milkshake to keep me company. But that's not professional. If you're on the trail, you stay on the trail. A lot can happen in twenty minutes, and never mind the odds. Or, if I could have got to a phone, I could have hired a stake-out. But the might-have-beens were for another day. Right now there was nothing to do but settle down to the kind of callouses, headaches and brain damage that are the career ailments of private detectives. I'm talking about the hours of waiting (too often in a men's toilet, not often enough in a lady's boudoir), the hunting and pecking, like some damned barnyard chicken, through a quart of dirt for a kernel of corn.

I threw the pack of cigarettes I don't smoke—except at times like this—on the seat beside me, lighted up and settled down. There was a sidewalk beside me and samples of condo life to parade it, lured from their shelters by the sunshine and heat: girls in shorts and halters; men in T-shirts and sweat; passing cars with windows open to catch a breeze; passing cars with windows closed and the air conditioning on; kids playing on the sidewalk, kids going inside for supper and coming out again.

In mid-June it takes a long time for night to fall, but fall it finally did, and I was there to witness the whole process. Cars started turning on headlights, children went into the condos and didn't come out again. Shadows deepened, streetlights came on, and the sky began to fade from blue to grey.

I planned to wait till half-past ten. If Shelly Polk hadn't come out by then, I could assign her as in for the night. Besides, it would be time to pick up Dana Doxey. Somehow, though, I expected something to happen before then. Shelly Polk didn't strike me as stay-at-home type.

So, at quarter of ten, just when it was really dark, a sleek yellow Cadillac, the last of the convertibles, swooped down the road and swung off to Shelly's condo. Behind the wheel was a young, dark-haired, husky stud who looked like something out of a thirties Cagney film. The car disappeared back of some buildings, there was a blare of musical horns, and in the time it takes a gold digger to say yes, out the car came again with blond and spicy Shelly, up to just above her bosom in a summer frock, her visible parts weighted with bracelets, earrings and rings, relaxing against the passenger seat.

How long had she said she'd been in town? Two weeks? That was some modelling school she attended.

They zipped out the condo gates on a speed run, and I almost lost them getting my car started. Then I picked them up at a traffic light six blocks down, and the rest was routine.

I tailed them to a roadhouse eleven miles out of town. It was a sprawling place with a parking lot that could hold the Orange Bowl and had been called Nero's Nest before the state police raided it for drugs and sex. Now a big neon sign identified it as Hugo's Hideway, but from the packing of cars in the lot and the line of people going in, I had to wonder if anything had been changed but the name. Given the price of gasoline, you aren't going to sucker the public into an eleven-mile drive unless the attraction is ultra high-powered. And drugs, sex and music, in that order, are three of the four biggest draws you've got. The other is gambling.

Shelly and her escort left the Caddy at the door, and I followed it when the attendant took it away to park. The hell with what Shelly and her guy did in Hugo's Hideway. I wanted the licence number of the Caddy.

When I got that, I went back to Frank's Bar.

CHAPTER EIGHT

Dana was doing her thing under the baby spot, knees and thighs peek-a-booing through her beaded string skirt, her white breasts quivering prettily. The place was packed, and the concentration was terrific. Even the women in the crowd—and there were more than you'd think—couldn't keep their eyes off her.

I ordered a tall rye and soda and worked my

way to the far wall, where I sipped and watched and looked around. Next to me was a blond youth, about Dana's age, in a plaid jacket. His eyes were as yellow as the glass of ginger ale he held, and he stared at Dana as if he didn't believe she was real. A passing patron bumped his arm and he slopped his drink, but he didn't notice. His eyes never left the dancing girl, and he acted catatonic. I watched her myself and I could almost understand. She had that whole room transfixed.

I left the yellow-eyed kid and worked a path through the customers to Dana's dressing room when she left the stage. She opened the door a crack when I knocked, and she said. 'I saw you. Don't worry, I won't run away.'

I took my drink back to the wall again and watched Lucille, the next go-go dancer, do her stint in a bikini bottom and no top. The yellow-eyed kid was gone and Lucille looked as if she was on drugs.

Dana found me there. She was dressed in spike heels and a form-fitting dress that revealed the shape of her bra hooks. 'All right,' she said, acting solemn and defensive.

I looked at her, I looked at Lucille, and I looked around at the crowded tables. 'There are three of you,' I said. 'Which is the third girl?'

Dana nodded at a nearby table, indicating the girl I'd guessed, a young brunette sitting with a middle-aged slob, she wearing a low-cut, gaping dress, holding a glass and showing too much interest.

'What's her name?'

'Sassie. Sassie Lejeune.'

'Don't any of you girls use your real names?'

Her look made me say, 'Never mind.' I put my glass on the nearest table and broke a path for her to the door.

We didn't eat at a greasy spoon. I took her to an after-the-theatre steak-and-brew joint, where the lights were dim but the menus were printed in English, and the prices wouldn't make her think I lied when I said I only wanted to talk. She was balky when I showed her the place, but when I said I hadn't eaten either and needed something substantial, she went along, but her feet were dragging.

She was stiff and defensive at the table, indicating she hadn't had much luck with men. Nor did she want to talk at first. She watched me sip a Manhattan but wouldn't take one herself. She feared it would lower her guard.

She did have a beer when the steak came. By then we'd gone through the salad bar, and she was beginning to fill an empty stomach.

Between the food, the beer and the fact I didn't stare at her cleavage, Dana began to relax, and though she wasn't one who smiled, she did start answering questions with more than yes or no.

She'd been go-go dancing at Frank's since last September, she said, and as far as she knew, it was a record. Most girls didn't stay long. If Ben Schill wasn't more than they could take, Jerry, the bartender, and the rest of the help were. You practically had to hide a ball bat behind the dressing-room door if you were to have your privacy. 'You saw how he walked you in on me this afternoon when I'd just got off the stage. He likes doing things like that, just to be mean.'

'Invasion of privacy?'

She nodded. 'There's a difference between parading around on a stage when you're half naked, and having a man in your dressing room when you're half naked. I don't know if you understand the difference, but Ben does. He pretends he doesn't. You tell him to knock it off, and he only laughs and says the guys he brings in aren't going to see anything they haven't already seen. And he's the boss. So you put up with it or you quit.'

'And most of the girls quit?'

'Not for that.' She shook her head. 'That's nothing. They quit because they don't like him

80

walking in and screwing them on the couch between acts any time he happens to get the idea.
And with him, every time he comes out his
office he's got a view of whoever's dancing,
so he gets the idea.'

'And that's what you have to put up with?'

'Not me. Not any more. I threatened to hit
him with a ball bat, and he leaves me alone.
Except for walking in to watch me dress—or
undress—things like that. I thought he'd fire
me, but I think he likes my body. I mean, I
think I bring in customers. But you have to
draw the line. If you don't, everybody's going
to be screwing you on the couch between
shows—Jerry, the kids who clean up...' Her
lip quivered. 'Lucille. They all gang up on
Lucille—except when I'm around. She's petri-
fied. She comes to work and she's shaking. I
tell her to get tough, but she's too frightened.
She's afraid Ben will fire her, and she'd rather
get raped than fired.'

'Ben was telling me you're all one big
happy family, except that he makes you
strip for everybody before you get hired.'

'Is that all he told you he makes us do?' She
snorted. 'We have to prove we can provide
complete service in case some of the customers
want to entertain us after hours. He doesn't
want the customers to get upset. At least

81

that's the story he gives us when he takes us on, but all our job includes is sitting with customers. Anything we want to do with them after is our own business.'

'He and everybody else leave you alone? What about—'

'*Now* they leave us alone. When you start out, though, they think they're onto a good thing and they'll do anything you let them do. It takes a while to learn how to get tough.'

'What about Nerissa? You were here ahead of her. Did she go through the same mill?'

'In the beginning. It was the same as with me. You show off what you've got, you let them take advantage of you, then you go to work. And when you can't take it any longer, you either quit or say "Enough." Or, as in Nerissa's case, somebody else says, "Enough." '

'The cop she went with?'

'That's right. Even Ben kept hands off once Matt Brent started coming around.'

'I understand the cop's wife didn't like it.'

'I'll say. She tried to beat me up one night just for sitting with him.'

'I heard about that. What happened?'

'All I was doing was sitting at his table, waiting my turn. We all knew him because he was Nerissa's guy, so since we had to mingle if business was slow or nobody was trying to hustle us, we'd drop down at his table and pass the time while Nerissa was up dancing.

'So one night, that's what I was doing, sitting with him, waiting my turn, when all of a sudden, out of nowhere, this broad attacks me, swinging a pocketbook and her fists and screaming names at me.'

'What'd she look like?'

'Tall, dark, mannish. I didn't get too good a look on accounta she was big and tough and I was trying to get under the table.

'Matt grabbed her and wrestled her out of there, and she practically went berserk. She was a real maniac.'

'What'd he say when he came back?'

'He didn't come back. We didn't see him after that for a week.'

'Did he ever explain what it was about?'

'Not to me. Like I say, it was a week or more before I saw him again, and he acted like it had never happened.'

'He never asked if she'd hurt you? He never apologized for what she'd done?'

She shook her head.

'But she *was* his wife?'

'That was the talk that went around. I don't know why else she'd attack me.'

'Would you know her if you saw her again?'

'Probably not. I didn't get a real look at her.'

'Do you think she attacked you because she thought you were Nerissa, or because you were sitting with him?'

'Because she thought I was Nerissa. She called me Nerissa. She called me a few other things, too. But Nerissa was up dancing. We were waiting for her to finish her gig.'

'The wife didn't know what Nerissa looked like, then?'

'I guess not. She just got hysterical about him and other women. I hear she killed him on accounta Nerissa.' She shook her head. 'No wonder Nerissa took off. You wouldn't get *me* involved in anything like that.'

'That's why she left? She tell you that?'

Dana shook her head. 'She didn't say anything to me. I just assume that.'

'You were working that night. What happened?'

'I was working the five-to-one shift, I and Lucille. Nerissa was three-to-eleven. Ben starts the entertainment at three and closes at one. So one of us is on there alone the first couple of hours, and it's fifteen minutes dancing, ten minutes rest. From five till eleven there're three of us, and for the next couple of hours we rotate and give the customers fifteen minutes of dancing with five-minute breaks. Then from seven o'clock on, we rotate fifteen minutes on, thirty

84

off, and you don't step down from that platform until the next girl is ready to step up,
so it's continuous.

'Then, from eleven till one, there're two girls
and we go back to rotating fifteen on, and five-
minute breaks between. And, of course, in between times we hop into a dress and mingle
with the customers.

'Naturally we aren't allowed to leave the
joint—except Nerissa. When Matt came by for
her, they'd go off together. Most of the time
she'd be back in time for her gig, but now and
then she was late, and we were left hanging up
there wondering when the hell she was going
to relieve us. I want to tell you, fifteen minutes
of gyrating up there on that platform is plenty
long enough. When the air conditioner's on,
it gets damned chilly even if you're moving.
And other times, you start to perspire and
that's even worse. You aren't going to look
very sexy if you're dripping sweat off your
nipples.'

Dana shook her head, lighted a match from
the book in the ashtray, watched the flame,
blew it out and dropped the match. 'So what
am I talking about things like that for? You
want to know about Nerissa's last night.'

I leaned close and interrupted. 'When you
get a chance look at the young guy two tables

away with the blond hair, yellow eyes and plaid jacket, eating alone, and tell me if you know him.'

She nodded and lighted another match while I had some beer. She dropped that match and said, 'I've seen him around. Why?'

'He's watching us. And he was in Frank's Bar when we left.'

'He hangs around Frank's. I've seen him there a lot. He's got those funny eyes. They look like lemons. He stands in the back and watches me dance.' She shivered. 'But I don't know him.'

'He ever bother you?'

'No. He just stares. He never says anything, he just looks at me with those scary lemon eyes. He makes me feel haunted.'

'Well, when we leave, I'll make sure he doesn't follow us anymore.'

Dana lighted and dropped another match, and her face was flushed. She was nervous now, and it was hard for her not to sneak glances at Lemon Eyes. 'Where were we? Oh, yes, I was telling you about that last night—Nerissa's last night. There was nothing special about it. I didn't know she'd quit until Ben came into the dressing room around midnight after one of my gigs and told me he was rearranging the schedule, that Nerissa was gone and Lucille and I would have to fill in for her till he could get a replacement.'

'Nerissa never even said goodbye?'

'Not a word. And it's a funny thing. We'd been roommates.'

I perked up. 'What's that? When?'

It had been a year ago. They'd both come to town trying to become actresses, and they'd shared a room while they starved and struggled and failed. In September Dana had answered an ad for a go-go dancer and stopped going hungry. Nerissa had sneered, but the following month, when the next opening came up, Nerissa was first in line.

'You stopped rooming together. Why?'

'She took up with some rich guy and wanted a better place, somewhere where she could entertain, if you know what I mean. I think he staked her, but I wouldn't know. Nerissa wasn't a talker. He came to Frank's a few times, but she never even introduced him. When she went with Matt, we all got to know him. But the rich guy she kept to herself.'

'You don't know his name and you don't know what happened between them—why he stopped coming around?'

Dana shook her head.

'Would anybody else?'

'She wouldn't talk to me and I roomed with

her, so I don't think so. I told her about myself, my childhood, things like that, but she wouldn't even say where she came from. You'd ask and she'd say, "I don't want to talk about it." ' Dana leaned closer. 'Look, can we go now? I've told you all I know about Nerissa, and that guy is still here.'

'You mean Lemon Eyes?'

She nodded. 'He gives me the creeps.'

I took Dana out of there and drove through enough side streets to make sure Lemon Eyes wasn't on our tail. After that I took her home. Home to Dana since she and Nerissa had split up was a small apartment building on one of the iffy streets in town, seedy, but not downright shabby. It was in a reasonably safe neighbourhood, meaning the muggers weren't loitering against the lamp posts.

I took her to the front door, which was at the head of half a dozen granite steps flanked with iron railings. We stood for a minute under the light, and she looked cute and pale and pathetic all at the same time. Her high spiked heels and her skin-tight dress made me think of a little girl in grown-up clothes. In fact, the dress was so tight I thought she'd be afraid to eat lest she split it open.

She held her purse in front of her and prepared to resist whatever I might do beyond kissing her good night. I'm too old for those games, and I didn't even proffer the expected kiss. Instead, I thanked her for her help and said I'd come back if I had more questions. She decided she was glad she could help and she really had enjoyed the meal.

I said that was nice, bade her good night and turned to go.

She said in disbelief, 'You really mean it, don't you?'

I was already down a step when I stopped. 'Mean what?'

'That you'd buy me a meal without making a pass.'

'Sure. Why not?'

Now she was getting unstrung. There she was, primed to fight for her virtue, and the battle wasn't joined. That the gentleman didn't even want to kiss her was almost an affront. She had a cute little figure and was used to being leched after. 'You're different,' she said. 'I'm not used to men like you.'

'We're not all carbon copies of Ben Schill.'

She thought for a moment, compressing her lips in the shadowy light from the wrought iron overhead. 'I suppose, since you *are* a gentleman, it would be safe to invite you up for a nightcap...if you didn't stay too...didn't mistake my intention. It's only a studio apartment and it's cramped, but it's pleasant, and it's the least I could do.'

Ah me, the old boy-girl game. She wanted to be safe, but not too safe. She had the need to tempt danger. It's so hard for people to let well enough alone.

I smiled and shook my head. 'Thanks, but no thanks. Right now you're safe. But if I came up to your studio apartment you wouldn't be safe. You wouldn't be safe at all.'

I gave her a wave and trotted on down the steps, leaving her looking after me thoughtfully —and maybe wistfully? It was hard to see her expression in the shadows when I glanced back.

There were trees on the street, large-boled maples thick enough to hide behind. Someone was behind the nearest one, and he sprang out at me. It was Lemon Eyes, and he had something heavy in a raised hand. 'You're going to stay away from her,' he said in low, hot-lead tones. He called me a filthy, dirty minded whoremonger, and a few other names as well, but I didn't catch the rest because I was throwing up a protective arm and trying to duck the thing in his hand he meant to crush my head with.

The trouble was, he had me off guard, and I was caught cold. My head exploded in a shock of pain and a shower of stars, and that was that.

CHAPTER NINE

Smart me. I made sure Lemon Eyes didn't follow me to Dana's pad, without ever stopping to think he might already know where she lived. A great detective I am. Sometimes I wonder why people hire me.

So there I lay, flat on my back on the sidewalk. I'd been unconscious, but I don't think for long—I don't recall hitting the pavement, but I remember the sound of his running feet and the clatter of spiked heels coming down the steps. Dana says she shrieked. I didn't hear that either. All I knew was her on her knees beside me, trying to turn me over, and I, thinking as I turned that she was raising hell with her panty hose kneeling on the concrete like that.

I said, 'I'm all right, it's all right,' so she wouldn't worry too much. She felt where I got hit and I said, 'Ouch.'

'You're not bleeding,' she told me, 'but there's this terrible swelling.' She helped me sit up and pulled my head against her breast and cradled me. My head was splitting, but she still felt and smelled awfully good. I didn't try too hard to get up.

'Who was it?' she said. 'Was it that man... with the yellow eyes?'

I said it was. 'He already knows where you live.'

She nodded. 'I thought so. I've seen him in the neighbourhood. He's usually behind a tree or something.'

'I wish you'd told me. We could have saved that detour—and maybe my skull.'

'Can you stand? I've got to get you up to my place.'

'I can stand. He didn't hit me that hard.' I let her help me up to prove it. I put a hand against the tree. 'Just get me to my car.'

'You can't drive. You're crazy.'

'I've got aspirin in the glove compartment. I'm ready for all emergencies.'

'You're coming upstairs. You aren't going home like this. It's my fault you got hit.'

She took me by the arm and guided me. I didn't fight her. I'm dumb, but not that dumb. When the plot thickens, you put on your boots and wade in, you don't go home and turn on the TV.

Dana's studio apartment was a ten-by-fifteen room with a window into an air shaft on the right, a daybed to the left, a small stove, sink, tabletop icebox behind a curtain at the far end, and, behind the kitchen, a bathroom designed for midgets. There was a table, a couple of chairs, dresser, a rock'n'roll poster over the daybed, and a closet almost big enough to hold a change of clothes.

Dana helped me onto the bed, propped me with cushions and went to get water and her own aspirin. On the dresser, facing me, was a framed, full-length colour photograph of Dana in an artistic pose, one knee flexed, head turned to a bowed profile, arms forming a circle above, fingers delicately poised. It was all very arty except she was totally nude.

She brought me the medication, and when I thanked her I indicated the picture. 'I forgot my glasses,' I said.

'Oh, that. That was when I was nineteen. I had some studies made. I thought maybe I could become a porno movie star. I mean, that's one way to become a star.'

I said, 'I gather the only difference from the other way is you do it *on* camera.'

'I quit,' she said. 'It was worse than go-go dancing. Everybody got into the act, even the kid who went out for coffee. All they wanted was the porn, never mind the stardom. It was all off camera.'

'Girls have it tough,' I said.

'That's right.' She sat down beside me. 'I know you're only saying that, but it's true. Sure we get all kinds of special favours from men because we're girls, but we have to ante up eventually or we're going to get shafted.'

'Except you've got Ben Schill trained.'

She shivered. 'Yeah, but when you think what I had to go through to get to that spot!' She looked at me. 'You know something? You know the only reason you're up here? And I mean regardless of your getting hit—I mean why I didn't just put you in your car and let you drive home the way you wanted?'

'Because you felt responsible for Lemon Eyes bopping me?'

She shook her head. 'I only brought you up here because you didn't try to make me let you come up. You didn't try to force your-self on me.'

'That doesn't make a lot of sense.'

'Sure it does. I was all set to fight.'

'I promised you I wouldn't make a pass.'

'Sure you did, and I found out all about men's promises when I was thirteen years old. You're the first man I've met in ten years who stood by it.'

'The only reason is that I've got a head-ache.'

She laughed. She got up and brought the picture over, sat down with me and held it on our laps. 'You know something,' she said, 'I've always liked this picture. If I do say so myself, I was a damned good-looking broad at nineteen.' She admired the picture for a bit and said, 'Do you know, I've only put on three pounds since that was taken?'

'Where?'

She burst out laughing. 'I thought you had a headache.'

'I'll tell you what,' I said. 'Give me two more aspirins and fifteen minutes and check back.'

'You're on.' She left me with the picture and went off with the water glass.

CHAPTER TEN

I didn't get out of bed until ten the next morning, but I can't say I was rested. There was the injury I'd suffered, there was all the aspirin I'd taken, there was the fact that the studio couch was cramped with the two of us on it and, while Dana was nice to sleep beside, cuddling up to her was a distraction. In addition, she was frisky. She hadn't had sex for fun, she said, since she was seventeen, and even then she was nervous because it was in a car and she was afraid of the cops. This time, the only hang-up was my headache and she didn't feel that at all.

So, as I say, by the time I pulled myself together and looked at a clock, I was already an hour late for the office, and I felt as if I hadn't gone to bed.

Dana was still sprawled out under the covers, sleeping like a baby. Her workday didn't start till three, so she had no conscience. I groped my way to the wall phone beside the door and dialled the office. Eileen said, 'I was beginning to wonder about you. Is everything all right?'

I said I'd had a slight accident and there'd be a little delay, and what was the early morning report?

'How slight?'

'A bump on the head. Mild, purplish swelling. No blood, no concussion.'

'Is it the "I walked into a door" kind?'

'What kind is that?'

'That's code for "I got slugged from behind." '

'Oh.'

'That's the kind, isn't it? Knowing you,

you don't get hit on the head any other way.'

'I'm supposed to be the detective in this outfit. You're supposed to do chores.'

'I don't do windows.'

'But you can dial the MVD. You can get me the name and address and make of car that goes with licence plate number AM9687.'

She repeated it back and said, 'Where do I call you?'

'I'll be in for it. I'll pick it up.'

'The "Don't call me, I'll call you," stuff?'

'You're full of questions this morning.'

'This job you hired me for leaves me in limbo. I'm just trying to orientate myself.'

'You find out who owns that car and we'll both orientate.'

She sighed and said, 'A girl feels so lucky to work for bosses who have such snappy comebacks. She lies awake at night wondering if they're going to survive. How's the head your door walked into? Have you had your skull X-rayed?'

'They haven't developed the X-ray machine that can pierce my skull. Get to the MVD will you? I don't want to get hit on the head again.'

She said, 'Yes, sir,' with the proper hint of panic.

I made bacon, eggs and coffee from what was in Dana's little icebox and on the cabinet shelves over the stove. Then I woke her up, told her to put something on and come to breakfast. She sat up in bed, stretched, yawned and made faces. 'It's too early to eat. It's not twelve o'clock yet.' Then she said, 'What's the matter with you? You're all dressed.'

'My workday starts ahead of yours. I'm about to eat and run.'

She pulled my hand against her breast. 'You don't really have to go to work. Stay around for a while.'

I kissed the top of her head. 'Staying around would be fun, but it wouldn't pay the rent. Now, do I eat alone, or are you going to eat with me?'

She decided she'd eat with me and sat down at the table. I got a dressing gown out of her closet and draped it over her shoulders. 'Pretty girls ought to wear clothes when they eat breakfast.'

She sulked. 'Most men like to see me in the nude. They pack Frank's Bar for it.'

'And you think if you don't wear anything, I'll forget to go to work. But it's not going to happen. So don't you think it'd be better for your morale if you didn't try?'

She slipped her arms into the robe then and tied it about her waist, but she didn't like not getting her way. She pitched into her breakfast and said, 'When am I going to see you again?'

She was forthright if nothing else. I said I didn't know, it depended on my work.

'Looking for Nerissa?'

'That's my work.'

'Maybe I could help you. You know, ask people about her? Keep my ears open?'

'Sure,' I said. 'Anything you hear, I'd like to know about.'

'You could pick me up after work at night and compare notes.'

Poor Dana. She couldn't wait to plan my future. I don't even know, when I get up in the morning, what I'll be doing that night, and she was trying to chart my course for the balance of Nerissa's disappearance. That's one of *les différences* between boys and girls about which I don't shout *'Vive!'*

'We'll see,' I said. 'I have to stay flexible. But there are things you could tell me that would help.'

'Anything.' She wiped bacon grease from the corner of her mouth with her paper napkin.

'You started work at Frank's in September, and Nerissa took the next opening in October...'

'That's right. I don't remember the date, but it was October.'

'What happened to her then? Tell me everything you can remember about her career in the bar before Matt Brent entered the picture. There was a rich guy, you say. What else do you recall? How did she go over? Did she have many dates? Tell me everything you can about her.'

Dana said, 'Well, she's pretty, and she has a good figure. I guess you can't deny that. And she got popular pretty fast.' Dana looked down the front of her robe. 'I don't think her figure is better than mine, but it's good.' She leaned elbows on the table. 'Which reminds me—what do you think of Lucille's figure? She's not as well developed as I am, and she sags a little. Don't you agree?'

'You're very sensational,' I said. 'And Nerissa's built like you?'

'Pretty much. She's a little taller.'

'And the customers went for her? Tell me about them.'

Dana leaned her chin in her hand, and her dark eyes grew reflective. 'Mostly,' she said, matter-of-factly, 'it was barflies buying her drinks and seeing how far she'd let them slide their hands under her skirt. You know, the ordinary kind of creep. But I don't think she ever went out with them after. There was one old guy who had dough, and he took a fancy to her and I think she might have gone out with him once. I didn't pay that much attention and, like I say, Nerissa didn't tell you anything.'

'Then there was the young rich guy with the flashy car who dated her a few times. That's the one I told you about, who made us stop rooming together. She went somewhere else and I came here.

'But he was a lemon. I don't mean she said so. She never said a word about him. But she only went with him a few times and he stopped coming around. Maybe she wouldn't do all the things he wanted her to, or maybe she didn't like him and preferred poverty.' Dana gave me a steadfast look. 'You know, sometimes, some of us girls can't be bought!'

'And you think that was the case with Nerissa?'

Dana gestured. 'Who knows? I wasn't rooming with her then. She didn't tell me anything when we did room together. What would she tell me now?'

'All right, what happened next?'

Dana cupped her chin in both hands and stared at the walls. 'Let's see, what then?' It came to her slowly. 'Then there was another guy. He used to buy her drinks and they seemed to have a thing going, except I don't know if he took her out. It was hard to say.

'But the reason I remember him is that Matt

Brent was a friend of his, and it was this guy who introduced Matt to Nerissa. And from then on, Matt took over and Nerissa was *his* girl.'

'Tell me about the friend. You remember his name?'

Dana had to shake her head. As in other things, Nerissa was reticent. Dana never met the man, nor could she describe him well other than to say he was about the same age as Matt, had darkish hair, ordinary face, ordinary clothes. He fitted the description of any Mr Anonymous.

'You say he introduced Nerissa to Matt? You say he brought Matt into the bar to watch Nerissa dance?'

Dana agreed. 'In fact, now that I think back on it, I was dancing when it happened. I remember this guy Nerissa used to sit with was there and Matt was with him. I didn't know Matt then, of course, so all I was thinking was, who's the guy with Nerissa's guy? And Nerissa went over to their table after I relieved her, and I remember noticing the two men standing up and Nerissa's guy making introductions. And she sat down next to Matt. I was only paying attention because I was surprised to see Nerissa's guy coming in with a friend.'

'And after that, Matt took over?'

'After that, it was all Matt. He went for her like a ton of bricks.'

'And what happened to the friend who made the introductions?'

'I never saw him again.'

'Would you know him if you did?'

'I might.' Then she smiled at me. 'I could ask Lucille if she knows him. You could pick me up after work tonight and I could—'

'I'll have to think about that,' I said. 'I don't want to give Lemon Eyes another shot at me.'

'He's a creep,' she said. 'He hangs around the bar and he watches my apartment. He never says anything. He just hangs around. I figure he's some kind of freak. Do you think I ought to call the cops?'

'Not yet,' I said. 'He may be trying to protect your virtue.'

'If he is,' she snorted, 'he ought to beat up on Ben Schill.'

'Has he ever given you trouble when other men have seen you home?'

'You're the only man I've *let* see me home. I don't want those creeps in the bar knowing where I live.'

'Know how Lemon Eyes found out?'

'He probably followed me. It wouldn't be all that hard if you wanted to go to the trouble.'

CHAPTER ELEVEN

I made some detours *en route* to the office. The first was to the home of John Oates, the neighbour who'd phoned the police that Matt Brent was dead.

He was at work, of course, and what opened the door was a shapeless woman in an old bathrobe, a mud pack and neat rows of pink hair curlers, who was shampooing the rugs wearing rubber overshoes. She gave me a quick up-and-down and said, 'We're not buying encyclopedias this year, sonny.'

Since I'd cracked the thirty barrier on my last birthday, you can see what generation she came from. I said, 'How're you fixed for Christmas-tree lights and get-well cards?'

'Oh,' she said. 'A live one. If I'd known I was going to be entertaining, I'd've put on more makeup.'

That sort of thing was fun, but it wasn't income-producing. I handed her my card and said, 'I'm really making a survey of murder and its motives.'

She peered at it and gave it back, wet and sticky. 'Do you honestly think I could read that without my glasses? I think you're trying to charm me into buying something.'

'I'm trying to charm you into giving me some information about the murder next door.'

'You mean when Carla Brent put the slug in her old man? Tell me, what's that card say?'

'It says I'm a private detective by the name of Simon Kaye.'

She leaned closer and squinted. 'The hell you say. You don't look like a detective. You look like a nice young lad working his way through college selling magazine subscriptions.'

'Now I think you're trying to charm *me* into buying something.'

'Look, come in and talk. I've got to keep shampooing the rug while it's still wet. If you want to take off your shoes and socks, you can shampoo it for me.'

'Sorry. Vacuum cleaners is my line. But I would like to talk...hear you talk, that is.'

'You don't want to listen to an old woman blab. You oughta wait till my husband gets home. He can tell you more about Matt and Carla Brent than I can. He's the one who went over there when we heard the shots. I told him he was a damned fool. You butt into a shooting and you're apt as not to get shot yourself. But he was smart. He'd counted the shots. Six of them. He knew the gun was empty.'

'What'd the shots sound like?'

'Like a gun going off. Guns have that special kind of "whammo" sound, if you know what I mean. I was once a WAC, so I've heard guns. You wouldn't believe I was ever a WAC, would you? You wouldn't believe I was ever that young, would you? But if you go back far enough, even the oldest of us were young.'

'Look, if you want the Grandmother of the Year Award, you have to talk to the tournament chairman.'

'My mistake. I thought you *were* the chairman.'

'That's next year. Getting back to the shooting, bringing your WAC training to bear on the matter, how were the shots spaced? Tell me your reaction.'

'Well, let's see about that. My Johnny and I were playing canasta. You'd like my Johnny. You're as looney as he is. So all of a sudden, there's this explosion. And we look at each other and say, "What the hell was that?" Then we thought, "Was it Matt Brent's gun?" Then it goes off again. And again. And it keeps going off. And my Johnny jumps up and says, "I'm going over there," and off he scoots. I tried to tell him he was crazy but,

106

as I mentioned before, he'd counted the shots, and he knew it'd take a while for whoever was shooting to reload.'

'And Carla met him at the door?'

'That's right, and she said, "Matt's dead, you can't come in," or something like that, and she blocked the door. So Johnny ran back here and phoned the police. First, of course, he told me Carla had killed the guy.' Mrs Oates shook her head. 'Can't say I'm surprised. Not the way they used to scream at each other. It spoiled the summers for us, year after year. You couldn't open your windows. I don't know why two people get married if they can't get along together. Or, if they do get married, why they stay married. It's uncivilized. It's really un-civilized.'

'How long have *you* been married?'

She was pushing the shampooer back and forth over the rug, a shapeless figure of a woman, made up to look like Gargantua, yet there was something interesting and attractive about her.

'Would you believe forty years?' she answer-ed grinning. 'We met in the army. Last week was our anniversary. We held our uniforms in front of us and stood in front of the mirror to repeat our vows. We used to tuck some of us back into our uniforms, but not any more. It'd be like getting back into your baby clothes. We've outgrown those days and, to tell the truth, we wouldn't have it any other way.'

'Do you know what the Brents used to fight about?'

'Sure. Everything! If he said the sky was blue, she'd say it was green. If she wanted coffee, he wanted tea.'

'It's claimed she killed him over another woman. Would you know anything about that?'

'If Nerissa is a woman's name, then it was about a woman. I don't know how you spell it, but the pronunciation was loud and clear.'

That was all she could tell me about Nerissa, and I explored the next logical track. 'You were neighbours of the Brents. Obviously, they weren't close...'

'Obviously! Who wants to be in a boxing ring all the time?'

'Who were their friends?'

Mrs Oates's laugh had a raucous note. 'Now listen, you clean-cut college-type kid, you've got to get out of your ivory tower. Couples like that don't have mutual friends. You don't say, who were *their* friends? What you ask are, who were *his* friends, and who were *her* friends? It's like separate towels and separate toothbrushes—and separate bedrooms, if you get what I mean.'

'And who were *his* friends, then?'

'Cops. Only cops.'

I thought a moment. Had a *cop* introduced Matt Brent to Nerissa Claire? 'What cops?' I asked. 'Do you know any names?'

She laughed and shampooed and trod through the soapsuds like a kid in a puddle. 'You think they introduced us? How would I know? All I can tell you is that guys in uniform would come to the door and ride with Matt to work.'

'Did you ever hear the Brents mention any names besides Nerissa?'

'Yeah,' she said. 'You might ask about somebody named Jake.'

'On the police force?'

Mrs Oates laughed. 'Don't take me too literally, sonny. I'm an old hag who's forgotten how to fly my broomstick. The Brents were our neighbours, and we tried to be neighbourly—talked over the fence and all that, but we always made sure the fence was there. As the poet says, "Good fences make good neighbours," and that was the way for us to be good neighbours. The Brents never entertained, they never went out together, so far as we could tell, other than to a restaurant every few months and back home right after.

'But Carla yelled more than one name in

those fights they had. There was Nerissa, who seemed to be the heart of the problem, but there was also somebody named Jake, and she blamed Matt's whole problem on him.'

That helped. I wrote it down and said, 'Do you know anything more about Jake than just his name?'

Mrs Oates thought a minute. 'He must have a wife named Gail,' she said. 'Because I recall hearing Carla threaten to tell Gail that Jake introduced Matt to Nerissa.'

That was a worthwhile encounter, if on the *outré* side. My next stop was police headquarters to see what could be learned down there.

Dan Saxton was in and, for a change, available. I said, 'How was the raid?'

'What do you know about it?'

That meant it hadn't gone off successfully. I shrugged, 'Only that you haven't been able to crack the hot-car ring.'

He swore and said they hadn't been able to get a lead. 'Only two or three garages, repair or rental agencies are big enough to handle such an operation, and we can't find a clue to tie them in. That means the cars are being trucked out of town. And there's only one trucking company big enough for that, and they're clean too. But the cars still disappear off the streets. I don't know where they go.' He banged a fist on the desk and swore some more. 'Is that what you wanted to see me about?'

I said no, that was just a form of greeting. 'It's Matt Brent's murder. I hear you handled it.'

He said, 'Yeah. One of those unfortunate things. You play around, you take your chances.' He looked up at me. 'But his wife didn't have to shoot him. She could've got a divorce. What's your interest?'

I told him I was looking for the 'other woman.' 'Know what became of her?'

'We never saw her. We wouldn't have known there was another woman from what the wife told us. She kept saying a burglar killed her husband, she was innocent, she had no motive and all that crap. So we looked around and there was evidence of this Nerissa Claire all over the place, a note from her in Matt's wallet, an ad for the topless bar she danced in, souvenirs in his bureau drawers. We showed those to the wife, and she swore up and down she didn't know anything about it. Then we got it from the neighbours that she fought with Matt about the woman and we got it from the bar that she went down there and created a scene.'

'And Carla denied it all?'

'That's right. The neighbours were lying, it was someone else in the bar.'

'Know what happened to the other woman?' I asked him again.

'Only that she left town.'

'Know why?'

Dan shook his head. 'It's no concern of ours. We don't want her for anything. Neither does the prosecution.'

'You know if she quit her job before or after Matt Brent got murdered?'

Dan didn't know that one either.

'One last question. Is there a guy on the force named Jake?'

'Three of them.'

'This Jake has a wife named Gail.'

'That would be Jake Metter. You think he can help you?'

'I don't know, but I'd like to talk to him.'

Dan Saxton turned to the roster. 'I'll see if I can track him down for you.'

CHAPTER TWELVE

Jake Metter was off duty that day, and I caught him in his backyard working with a Simoniz can and a rag to make the hide of a pure-white, two-seater Porsche glisten in the sun. He was a five-year veteran, younger than I, but not by much, and so tall and broad in the beam the bucket seat behind the wheel looked too small for his bulk.

I told him my name as I came up the drive and was reaching for my licence when he shook his head. 'I heard of you,' he said. 'You used to be a cop—quit the force just before I came in.'

I offered my hand, but he said his was too dirty. He laid into the polishing again.

'Nice car.'

'Second-hand,' he answered. 'But it'll do.'

'Do what? About a hundred and fifty?' It might have been second-hand, but it could have stood on the showroom floor.

'Whaddaya want?' he asked while he worked. 'You investigating me?'

He obviously wasn't welcoming company this morning. I said, 'As a matter of fact, I'm trying to find somebody, and I understand you might know her.'

Jake Metter put down the cloth, stuck a deliberate hand down the front of his dirty T-shirt to produce a crushed pack of cigarettes, put one in his mouth, laid the pack on the fender without offering me one, then produced a book of matches that advertised the neighbourhood bowling alley, lighted the cigarette and laid the matches on the pack of cigarettes. 'So,' he finally said, exhaling a deep lungful of smoke, 'I might know the whereabouts of a missing girl, huh?'

He had an interesting way of putting it. 'I should be so lucky,' I said. 'I was hoping for a clue.'

'Who's the girl?'

'Nerissa Claire.'

He gave me a hooded look. Then he eyed the tip of his cigarette. When he looked at me again, he was scowling. 'Who the hell told you I knew a girl named Nerissa Claire?'

His tone was belligerent. It demanded an answer. But I was a cop myself—I made detective in fact—and I know the tactic. I said, 'You *do* know her, don't you?'

He tried again. 'I never heard of her.' He

looked me straight in the eye with daggers. 'I want to know who says I did.'

'You know *who* she is, don't you?' I answered. 'She's the girl Carla Brent shot her husband over.'

'Yeah! I still don't know her.'

'She used to be a go-go dancer in a place called Frank's Bar. You know the place?'

'No, I don't know the place.'

'It's on the main drag—big signs outside.'

'I don't mean I don't know the place,' he snarled. 'I mean I've never been in it.'

'The information I picked up is that you were the one who introduced her to Matt Brent.'

'Well, your information is wrong, buster. It must've been some other guy. And I'll tell you one other thing. I don't like you dumb private eyes coming around trying to smear people with wrong information.'

'What you're saying is, you don't go to topless bars?'

'I just told you.'

'Is that because your wife would object? What's her name—Gail?'

Jake Metter mashed his cigarette under his foot and jabbed a finger in my chest. 'Now I'm going to tell you one thing, smart boy. Get your ass outa here, off my property, and don't come back. If you want to make an enemy out of me,

I'll make you wish you were never born. I'll make you learn better than to pick on a cop.'

Getting jabbed in the chest with a thick finger is an event that makes me itch to blast a guy's jaw. He knew it, and he was baiting me. Let me start something in his own backyard and I'd end up in a jail cell. That's what he wanted, because I'd been baiting him too and he could barely keep from throwing a haymaker at me. I was trying to get him to say something, and he was trying to get me to do something.

So I took the jabbing finger and I even smiled. The anger drained away and I said, 'Well, who knows? Maybe my informant had the wrong man. Sorry to have bothered you.'

'You're goddamn right he had the wrong man. Next time check your facts before coming around making a fool of yourself.'

I went back to my car, deciding there must be more to him and Nerissa Claire than I'd been thinking.

When I returned to the office, Eileen was eating a sandwich and reading a magazine. 'I'm practising to be a receptionist,' she said. 'Tomorrow I'm going to bring in a kit and work on my nails.'

'Don't I give you enough to do?'

'The bills are up to the minute, the files are

116

in order, client reports are on your desk for your signature. All you've given me to do today is track down a licence number. How's the door you walked into?' She eyed me critically. 'You look a little lopsided, but otherwise normal.'

'And what did you get on the licence plate? Does the car belong to the head of the top modelling school in town?'

Eileen shook her head. 'Some detective. That's about as far off base as you could get.'

I was less than amazed. She said, 'You want to try for the silver medal?' and I said no, I just wanted to be surprised.

'The car,' she said, 'belongs to Vincent Manila.' She tore the sheet off the pad that bore the name and address. 'He's in the car-rental, parking garage, car-repair business. He models cars, not people.'

The address put Vincent Manila in the same part of town as the head of the modelling school, but not the same field of endeavour. Not by a city mile. I went into my office, folding the paper, putting it in my wallet and thinking about it. Vincent Manila? And the young stud behind the wheel of the car would probably be the son of Vincent Manila.

And how did he come to meet Shelly Polk in the two weeks she'd claimed she was in town?

That was only one of the questions that hovered over the case and contributed to the feeling there was more to Nerissa Claire's departure than an urge to get married the night her boyfriend got shot.

CHAPTER THIRTEEN

My next ploy in the Nerissa Claire case took place that evening. I went down to Frank's Bar at half-past eight. It was still light out, the kind of light that shows off topless dancers at their worst. At night, when it's dark and all you've got is a baby spot focused on a sexy dish making a stab at crowd seduction, there's a glamour to the scene. The dish looks sexier than a Hollywood boudoir. None of her scars and blemishes show, the costume covers the worst and exposes the best of her, and the spotlight tints her skin a colour that's better than skin.

In the bright hours of the afternoon, where the sun gets in, even with painted windows there's still excitement. The girls may be hued by day as well as by the spot, and it may take them off the pedestal and make them look human, but they still look edible.

It's only when the daylight is fading, but still has dying gasps to it, when it still trickles through the doors and windows and tells the barflies about home and family and bedtime for children, that the topless girls, shimmying and shaking their breasts, seem lacklustre and tawdry. Perhaps family time is not sex time, and the day's parting message is telling you so.

Dana was on stage, near the end of her stint, and she had reached that anticlimax period, where you could tell by the glaze of her eye that she was doing a countdown to break time.

I ordered a Scotch and soda and made sure she saw me, then went down to her dressing-room door. As soon as she got off the platform and through the escape corridor, she opened it and let me in. She was wearing her see-through cape, but she didn't let it get in her way. As soon as the door was closed again, she was in my arms, pressing warm, full breasts against me, locking her arms around my neck and kissing me in ways that meant we were supposed to use the couch. 'I knew you'd come,' she whispered when our lips parted enough for speech.

That's all very thrilling and enticing and hard to resist, but it's also a mite disturbing, for it takes your mind off business. She had a way of clinging that strenuously insisted that we not let go of each other until certain developing erotic appetites had been sated.

It was tough, but I fought the urges. 'Hey, sweetheart,' I said when I could sneak words between her lips. 'I have an assignment for you.'

'Great,' she said, thrusting her tongue between my teeth. 'What do I do? I mean, what do I do after we make love?'

She was still trying to get me down on Ben Schill's casting couch. Unfortunately, larger duties beckoned. 'I want you to go someplace with me,' I murmured against her lips. 'Between now and your next show. How much time do we have?'

Her ardour cooled. She knew now we were going to have to wait. She pulled back enough to look into my face but not enough to disengage the rest of us. 'I've got half an hour,' she answered. 'I could stretch it to forty minutes if the others will cover for me.'

'Question. Yes or no. You saw the guy who introduced Nerissa to Matt Brent. You watched him do it. Would you know him if you saw him again?'

'Oh, gee, Simon, I don't know.'

'If I showed you a bunch of people, and he

was one of them, do you think you'd know it?'

All she could say was, 'Try me,' which could be taken in any number of ways and which prompted me to tell her I'd do just that and we'd be back before her next show.

'Where're we going?'

'To a neighbourhood bowling alley.'

'Why?'

'Because I want you to take a look at the people bowling and see what kind of responses you get.'

'What are we going to do afterwards?'

'I bring you back here.'

'I mean when I finish dancing?'

'Your place or mine?'

'Now you talk the right language. Let's try yours next time.'

That's one of the hazards of the occupation. But we *do* have to go after information, don't we?

The bowling alley I took her to was the one advertised on the matchbook Jake Metter lighted cigarettes with. Wednesday night was bowling-league night and as the matchbook suggested, Jake and his wife were in the league. I say his wife because I checked out the place before I picked up Dana, and she was with him. The two of them would be sliding balls down the alleys most of the evening, and there'd be plenty of chance for Dana to do a make on Jake if she could.

I brought her in in her spiked heels and her sit-with-the-customers costume—a satiny, low-cut gown, which gaped where it didn't hug. It was sleeveless, backless and halfway front-less, and when we stood at the rear of the hall by the vending machines, looking at the men and women in their bowling outfits, their pant suits and low-heeled shoes, she said, 'I stick out like a sore thumb.'

I said, 'You stick out, but sore thumb isn't the way you do it.'

There were sixteen lanes in the broad low building, and the 'thwack' of ball against pins and the clatter as pins fell was a constant background noise. I said, 'Now I'll tell you what I want. You said you thought you might recognize the guy who introduced Matt Brent to Nerissa. I want you to see if anyone here looks like him.'

I let her stand and get her bearings. Jake Metter and his wife were on lane number four. The wife, Gail, a chunky young girl who could really zip that ball, was up, and Jake was minding the score sheet. The other couples at lanes three and four were sitting on the benches and working number three. I didn't say anything, just let Dana take her time.

All lanes were busy, and the place was alive. Guys heading for the lobby and the lavatories were eyeing Dana like Santa Claus had come to the wrong place and a little early.

Dana looked at me uneasily. 'I don't know,' she said. 'There're so many people.'

'No hurry. Why don't you walk closer? Circulate behind the benches. Start at lane one.'

She did, and I watched from the vending machines. Metter's back was to her and she passed him by, strolling to the end as if wondering what the game was all about.

The interesting thing is that though she didn't see him, he saw her. He turned from the score sheets as she was casing the first two lanes, and he gave her a double take. I mean he looked, and looked again, and it wasn't because she was wearing such a non-bowling outfit or because she was such a nifty dish, but because he'd seen her before. He stared and stared. I couldn't see his mouth, but I knew it was hanging open.

Then she turned his way, and he bent over the score sheets fast. He didn't know why she was there and he didn't know if she'd recognize him, but he wasn't taking chances.

She came back slowly, shrugged off a pickup

play, and passed him by again. He sneaked a following glance, and he was sore. He knew she was looking for him, but he didn't know why. But he was also damned well going to find out.

I gave her the high sign when she turned my way, and she broke off and came over. 'Did I do something wrong?'

I drew her into the lobby and was going to tell her to work that section over again, but before I could begin, Jake Metter came stalking through the entrance to see where she was heading and whom she was with.

He thought she'd kept going, and I wasn't expecting him, so it was surprise, surprise, and there we all were, stumbled together and gaping at each other. If there was a startled expression on his meaty face, I must have looked like a harpooned whale. Dana was stunned as well, but not so rattled that she couldn't point a finger and say, 'He's the one!'

There was a moment there when I thought this was my last day on earth. Everything in his face spelled murder. With the rest of us, we have to think about consequences if we kill someone. We also have to have the means. With him, it was different. He was a cop, and he carried a gun on his hip. The means were at hand. And if he lost his head and used it, he'd be excused in a hundred ways. Right or

124

wrong, cops protect each other.

On the other hand, he had his own deterrents. He couldn't arrest me, for I hadn't done anything. If he beat me up, I could sue. And if he killed me outright, well, even cops aren't immune from punishment. They might not let him bowl anymore.

All in all, he fought his temper and tried not to yell too loud when he said, 'What're you doing here? What the hell do you think you're doing?'

These words were directed at me, of course. He was ignoring Dana now, pretending he didn't know who she was.

I said, 'I don't know if you've met Miss Doxey? She's a friend of mine.'

He continued to pretend she didn't exist and thumped my chest with a finger that felt like a mallet. 'I warned you to stay away from me,' he announced in basso profundo tones to everyone around. 'You think you're a smart ass. You think you can cross me? Now you're gonna be sorry.'

He spoke with booming authority, and he was speaking in front of his friends. They looked at me as if I'd mugged my grandmother. This isn't to say I'd've been lynched, but I was disadvantaged. So I said, in as loud a voice as his, 'What have you done with Nerissa Claire?

Where are you hiding her?'

That had an interesting effect. It cowed him. The crowd's eyes brightened, but he shrank. His wife was back at lane four, but she'd be drifting this way if the noise kept up. If he wasn't afraid of me, he sure as hell was afraid of her.

'Get out of here,' he told me in a hoarse guttural. 'Beat it, both of you. And don't either of you ever come near me again!'

So much for that. My life was saved. The crowd opened a path to the door, and I walked it with Dana. Little Gail Metter was back there knocking down pins, but she'd got us out of the place unharmed. The chances were, though, that the name Nerissa Claire would get back to her before her husband did.

CHAPTER FOURTEEN

I walked Dana through Frank's Bar to her dressing room in case Ben Schill tried to give her a hard time. She wasn't late, but she'd left the premises, and that was a no-no in Ben's book. He wanted the customers buying her shots of tea.

Nerissa's replacement, Sassie Lejeune, was doing the topless bit this time. She was big in the breast department and flopped around a lot.

Ben wasn't around, and Dana felt free to give me an ardent kiss at the door. I said, 'Better watch it. Lemon Eyes is looking.'

'Oh God, is he here?'

'Against the wall in a corner. And he's got eyes for no one but you.'

'The hell with him. He's not going to scare me any more.' She gave me another kiss, the hello kind not the goodbye kind, and whispered she'd see me later. When I threaded my way back through the darkened room, Lemon Eyes had switched his attention from Dana to me, and his baleful yellow gaze followed. The bouncing girl on the platform was wasting her wares on him.

I went outside, joined the scattering of people wandering the sidewalks of our town's garish midway area, and stopped by the alley at the end of the building to light a cigarette. I didn't need to tarry long, for Lemon Eyes was pretty quick. He was out of the bar looking for me before I threw away the match.

I let him see me stroll into the alley, enjoying the cigarette. Once inside, I stopped, put my back against the wall and threw the cigarette away. Sure enough, in another second, Lemon Eyes was after me, and it wasn't a blunt instrument he was carrying tonight, it was a switchblade.

He came in fast, for he thought I was twenty feet ahead of him. In fact, he was in such a hurry, he didn't even see me until I clamped a hand on his wrist and wheeled him headfirst into the wall.

The switchblade clattered to the cement, and he went down with it. He would have spread out full-length, except I still held his wrist and my guide hand was still under his arm. As a result, he only went to his knees, and he moaned. He didn't know where he was or what had happened.

That was what I wanted. Now I let him go and gave him a kick that flattened him out. Any sonuvabitch who comes after me in dark alleys with a switchblade isn't going to earn a lot of good will. I don't know if I broke any of his ribs or not, but he's damned lucky I didn't kick him in the face. He'd have worn a different look for the rest of his life.

I pocketed his switchblade and gave him a fast frisk while he dreamed his dreams. He was carrying a blackjack in his side pocket, and I guess that's what he hit me with last night, for he had no other weapons. There was a wallet and the usual items—keys, change, handkerchief, etcetera.

I carried the wallet out to the light to see what he had. According to his papers, his name was Richard Loomis, his address was a mile and a half from where Dana lived, and he had two shirts at the cleaners. He carried about fifty dollars in cash but no credit cards.

I returned to the creep and stuffed his wallet back in his pocket. He was coming around now, moaning and trying to make sense out of things. I stood by and waited until he worked his way to his hands and knees, all the while groaning and holding a palm to his forehead.

Then I caught him by the collar, said, 'On your feet, hophead,' dragged him upright and planted him against the wall. The manoeuvre cracked his head against the bricks, and he started to cry. He wasn't a big man, maybe three inches shorter than I and fifty pounds lighter. It was like playing with a loaf of bread.

He took his hand away from his mashed forehead to look at the blood. He wasn't hurt that much, but scalp wounds bleed hard and he thought he was going to die. 'Help me,' he pleaded.

'Sure I'm going to help you,' I said and walked him deeper into the alley. We'd been making some noise, and passers-by were peering into the darkness, being careful not to be too curious.

He stumbled along, not wanting to go but having no choice. He was small, he was weak, he was groggy.

When I had him in so deep that nobody could see and hear, I banged him against the wall again and said, 'Now you're going to sing and dance, Mr Loomis. You're going to tell me all about Dana Doxey and what you're trying to do with and to her.'

He said he didn't know any Dana Doxey, and I whacked him across the chops. He said, 'Oh, you mean the go-go dancer?'

'How long have you known her, what do you mean to her—let's have all the purple prose.' I gave him another whack to get him started.

He tried to say he didn't know her, then allowed that he knew who she was and, yes, he did know where she lived. He'd found out her name, not by asking her, but by asking other people and listening to other people talk about her. He found out where she lived by following her home.

'Why?'

'I want to protect her.'

130

'From what?'

He shook his head to clear it and took a deep breath. 'From scum like you.' He started raging. 'It's bad enough that people look at her, but they lust after her. They want to act out their fantasies with her. They have no right to sully her with their evil desires.'

I said, 'Yeah? And what do you look at her for?'

His voice sobered and he grew very earnest. 'Out of appreciation for her beauty. Out of love and worship and respect. That's the only way she should be looked at—not with sinful lust, the way everybody else does.' His voice grew in intensity and dropped to a whisper. 'You think I don't see them? You think I don't watch what's in the eyes of the scum that sit in that bar and watch her dance? She is an artist, a thing of grace and beauty, and they stare at her with lust. God created the female form to be worshipped and adored, not to be lusted after.'

'So you thought you'd stick a knife between my ribs because I don't pray hard enough?'

'You take her home. You escort her. You hold her arm. You touch her! You, who aren't worthy to kiss the ground where she walks!' He struggled in my grip. 'You keep your filthy hands off her, you hear me?'

He was a pesky devil, and he tried to knee me. I smacked his head against the wall again. 'I don't want to get rough, junior,' I said, 'but I've got a message for you. *You're* the one who's going to stay away from that girl. And I mean starting right now. I've got another message. Don't let me see you again. Because if I do, I'm going to ram your head through the trunk of a tree.' I gave him a hard one across the chops. 'Do you get me?'

He tightened his lips and looked me in the eye.

I hit him again.

He took it without change of expression. He was telling me I could kill him and he wouldn't give in. He was like those religious freaks. They see the light and that's that.

That made it a standoff. Except that I couldn't admit it to him. So I gave him a left to the solar plexus, which dropped him to his knees and then onto his face. When I headed out of there, he was writhing slowly on the ground, clutching his stomach and retching.

Always leave 'em rolling in the aisles, I say. Except with him, it wouldn't do any good.

He'd be back.

CHAPTER FIFTEEN

So far this evening I'd made enemies out of Jake Metter and Richard Loomis, better known as Lemon Eyes. And the night was still young. No telling how big a score I could roll up.

With that in mind, I thought I'd circle by Shelly Polk's condominium to see if she had any lights on. She was another person who hadn't taken a shine to me on first meeting. If I shook her up a little on a second occasion, I might build her response into a violent dislike. Private detectives, like cops, don't generate much affection in the pursuit of duty. We're worse off than cops—we can't even give lost children ice cream cones.

Well, surprise, surprise. It was half-past ten, and the lights were on in Shelly's digs. And these weren't the lights you leave to make burglars think somebody's home. These were the lights you put on when you really *are* home. I scouted the premises and there was no shiny Cadillac in any of the parking spaces, so it looked as if Shelly was home all alone. It was worth a trip onto her stoop and a ring on her doorbell.

She opened the door as if she'd been waiting beside it, but it wasn't me she was waiting for. There she was in her party best, carrying an evening purse in her hand, and she was halfway onto the stoop before she realized she had the wrong date.

'What the hell!' she exclaimed with ice in her eyes, and back she leaped, trying to shut the door in the same motion.

Of course that didn't work because I had my foot in it, and since I was bigger and stronger, I pushed the door wider and got the rest of me in, too.

She came at me, clawing. I'm hell with the women, I am. I caught her wrists and walked her to the couch and sat her on it.

She stayed put, rubbed her wrists and glared at me as if I'd killed her cat. This was one of my bad nights. I couldn't intimidate a big man like Jake Metter, I couldn't intimidate a little man like Lemon Eyes, and now I couldn't even intimidate a young, helpless girl like Shelly Polk. The man upstairs will never renew my dragon licence.

'You're going to be sorry,' she said, giving me her smouldering look. 'You're going to be sorrier than you'd ever believe.'

'Why?' I said. 'Are you going to set your

134

friend Manila on me?'

She blinked. She didn't know how I'd heard about him. 'You're damned well right,' she said, accepting my knowledge.

'Tell me about him,' I said, standing over her. 'How'd you meet him?'

'Go to hell.'

'Not through modelling school,' I said chattily. 'He's in the car business.'

She glowered at me. 'How the hell do you know so much?'

'It's my business to know. And I want what you know. Where'd you meet him? How'd you meet him? You've only been in town two weeks—or so you claim. When did you move in here anyway? Tell me that part again.'

'I already told you,' she said. 'Leave me alone, dammit!' She was nervous now. Her breasts were heaving and the flimsy frock she wore didn't seem certain to stand the strain. Panic was rising, and that was interesting.

'I'm not going to leave you alone. Answer my questions.' I bent closer and she was intimidated now, all right. She was frightened to death.

'It was the first of the month,' she said. 'I told you that. The first of the month.'

'Where's Nerissa Claire?'

She shook her head. 'I don't know. She

135

went away. I told you that.'

'Where'd you meet Manila? Tell me where you met him.'

'I met him at modelling school. Tony came to modelling school. That's how I met him.'

'What's the name of the modelling school? I want to know what modelling school has your name on its lists.'

She was ashen now. 'You can't do that,' she whispered. 'It's against the law or something. Please. You can't do that.'

'Or maybe it wasn't at modelling school. Maybe he used to go with Nerissa. Could that be the answer? And he came to see Nerissa, only she was gone and you were here in her place?'

'Yes,' she said. 'That's it. That's what happened.'

'You agree a little too fast. Why don't you tell it to me instead of me telling it to you?'

She backed against the cushions as if I might strangle her. 'Yes, that's what happened,' she said. 'He used to know Nerissa and Nerissa ran away...'

'What for? Why did Nerissa run away?'

She squirmed. 'Please leave me alone. Nerissa ran away, I don't know why. You wanted me to tell you about Tony. Stop asking me about Nerissa. Tony came around to see her, and I said Nerissa ran away and he took me out instead.'

'What about this Matt Brent she was going with? What about him?'

She didn't just squirm now, she writhed. 'I don't know,' she said. 'I don't know about him.'

'Except that his wife shot him to death because he was seeing Nerissa. You know that, don't you?'

'I don't know.'

'It was in all the papers. Nerissa's name was there, too. What about it?'

'She used to see him. I knew that.'

'What was she doing—seeing Tony Manila too? Is that what you're saying?'

That was when a harsh voice behind me said to Shelly, 'Who's this punk?' and then, to me, 'What the hell do you think you're doing?'

And who should be standing in the doorway but Tony Manila himself, in a cream dinner jacket, maroon bow tie and pocket handkerchief, black trousers with a satin stripe, smelling of expensive cologne and looking like a store-window dummy.

Shelly Polk made a remarkable recovery. Instantly she was sitting up, straight as a virgin bride, saying to her white knight, 'I didn't tell him anything. Honest, honey, I didn't tell him a thing.'

'Who the hell is he?'

'That detective. He knows who you are.'

Tony advanced, eyes narrowed. 'So you think you can annoy my girl, huh?'

I said, 'I'm glad you're here. There're some questions I want—' It was a ploy that was supposed to disarm him or lengthen his fuse, or put him on the defensive or do something to slow his progress. Like a lot of my ploys, it didn't work. He speeded up and let go a right fist at my jaw. It wasn't a roundhouse right, either. It came in a small arc that carried his weight behind it and said he knew how to handle himself in a fracas.

Fortunately I do too, or he'd have rung down my curtain. I couldn't get out of the way of the punch—it was too well thrown. All I could do was ride it and it was some ride. I went into the wall, in a corner, knocking over an end table and lamp on the way. At the finish, I was on my backside but unhurt. In fact, the crack my skull got against the plaster was harder than the punch on the chin.

I was slow getting up. I thought I'd do better if he believed I was hurt. He might take pity on me, he might lose interest in beating me and opt for interrogation instead.

It wasn't my day. I couldn't guess right

about anything. He came at me with a relish that said he liked kicking cripples. There was going to be no help for it but to roll around with him and wreck Shelly's living room. I spun my body into his kick, catching his leg. That brought him down, and another end table flew, another lamp crashed. He kicked with his free foot and clawed for my eyes. I hit him in the jaw but couldn't get any leverage. With my other hand I tried to get hold of his throat.

The trouble was, he was as strong as I was, just about the same age, and just about as disciplined. I've got a black belt in karate and thirty-eight amateur fights behind me, so I expect to come out on top in the rough and tumble, but when it boils down to bear-hug wrestling, there's no chance for skill, and it's all a question of who's stronger or who's on top and has an arm free. Since, as I say, Tony was my equal in strength and conditioning, it was six to five and pick-'em brawl.

We clutched and rolled, and Shelly was by the door, ready to run if the wrong guy won. I kept struggling to get free. If I could regain my feet and set myself, then we'd see how long he could hang in there. But that wasn't his fight plan. He was after my eyes, and for that he had to be close.

I finally got loose by finding one of his nerve

points. He jerked away and I was up ahead of him. That was my chance, and I caught him with an uppercut kick under the chin as he was scrambling to his feet, and that put him into the same corner he'd knocked me. Like me, though, he was riding the blow and he wasn't hurt. Like me, he pretended he was, and lay waiting for me to come for him so he could kick me across the room. I resisted the invitation. I beckoned him. 'On your feet, you clown.' I was boiling, and that's not smart. You don't want to lose your temper around people like him. You forget to think.

Like now. Tony Manila hadn't put on his best clothes to have a fight in, and they were mussed enough. So when I held back and gave him breathing space, he slipped a hand inside his jacket and pulled out a gun. It was a small gun from a holster tucked so close to his armpit I had never felt it.

That changed the rules of the game. I stood still. Shelly Polk, who was half out of the door when Tony hit the deck, came back in and stared. The only one who moved was Tony. He got up slowly, tongue licking a cut at the corner of his mouth, the gun pointed dead centre at my chest, his dark eyes gleaming with hate and a touch of wildness.

I have to admit I didn't feel very good about

things just then. I didn't know what he planned to do—especially with that uncontrolled look in his eye. I didn't think he'd gun me down in front of a witness in his girlfriend's apartment. That's not something any sensible person would contemplate. But I didn't know how sensible this guy was.

Shelly didn't know either, for when he levelled his gun, she shrieked, 'For Christ's sake, don't shoot!'

He didn't tell her he wouldn't. He let us guess about that. For three seconds he kept that black muzzle pointing with icy steadiness. Then he said, with great reluctance, 'I'm gonna tell you something, Jack. If I ever see you again—if my girl ever sees you again—if you come nosing around again, this gun's going off. It's going to go off in your face. Turn around!'

I turned and faced the door. Manila came up behind and jabbed the gun in my back. 'Move to the door. One step at a time.'

The pressure of the gun went away. Now I didn't know where it was—not that I would have tried anything if I had. I was content to live and fight another day.

Shelly moved out of the way while I took slow steps to the door. I never made it. One pace short, he clubbed me from behind, and for the second time in less than twenty-four hours, I got bashed on the bean. A lesser skull would have given up. So would a smarter detective. There must be better ways to make a living.

When I awoke, I was lying in the open on soft cool ground with a starry sky above and a far-off streetlight for company. I was awhile getting my bearings—remembering what had happened to me and where, trying to decide my present status and why. My head ached. I was getting used to its aching. Every time it stopped, I got sapped again. This time, though, everything else ached as well. My whole body felt bruised and sore.

After about ten minutes, I had it all together. I was lying at the foot of the steps outside Shelly Polk's condominium. Apparently mannequin Tony Manila, in his creamy rich clothes, had, after knocking me cold, kicked me out the door and off the stoop.

When I could turn my head enough, I looked up at the windows. All were dark. Shelly had been waiting for Tony to pick her up. They had a late date, and I guessed they were still on it.

I looked at my watch. Three o'clock. If I'd been unconscious that long, I wouldn't be able to focus on my watch. Part of the time I must have slept—my body doing double duty; healing me and at the same time trying to keep me out of trouble. Let me stay awake long enough, and I'd do myself in.

I sat up and my body ached more than my head. At least no bones were broken. Tony Manila missed a bet there. If he'd cracked a shin, he could have made sure I stayed away from his girl.

In time I got to my feet and found I could walk. When I started my car, I found I could drive. I made the car take me alll the way home to my own condo. I parked it in the slot back of the stairs to the enclosed entry to where my condo sits over the garage I never use.

I slowly climbed the steps to the storm porch and was about to enter it when a sleepy voice said, 'It's about time. I thought you were going to stand me up.'

It was Dana Doxey.

CHAPTER SIXTEEN

Dana made breakfast in the morning. That's not because I was helpless, for I was in good shape, considering. My head was swollen and my body sore, but they didn't ache more than a couple of aspirins' worth, and I was fit to face the day. Dana, however, was being domestic. She made toast, coffee, scrambled eggs, bacon, dried cereal with cut-up bananas on it—the works.

That's not the way I handle my breakfast menu, but it's the way she wanted it handled, and I went along. She even had the morning paper folded at my place, and she wore one of my bathrobes with the sleeves rolled up enough to let her hands show. It was very housewifey— which was what it was supposed to be—just the kind of thing that makes me nervous. Dana was very cute and very sexy and she was a lot of fun for a romp around the bedroom even if you have a headache, but I don't know where else we'd be compatible. Neither did she. But she seemed more interested than I in finding out.

It was tough for her, getting up at my hour in the morning, but she braved it through, stifling her yawns and smiling through her sleepiness. She was all in favour of kissing me goodbye and sacking out until noon, but if I let her follow that script, she'd be back on my doorstep again tonight—with her suitcase.

I told her that was no go, this was not her lodge. Then she wanted to know about tonight. After all, I'd stood her up last night. Shouldn't I make it up to her?

I said, 'Listen, I'm working on a case. My time's not my own.'

'Couldn't I work on it with you? Didn't I help you last night?'

'Yes, and you might help me again, but—'

'How?'

I patted her cheek. 'Don't be so eager, luscious. The detective business is the pits. You've seen what's happened to me, haven't you?'

'I don't mind, if I can take care of you.'

'But I mind. I don't like getting zonked on the noggin.'

'But you said I can help. What do you want done?'

'You told me that before Jake Metter came around there was another guy interested in Nerissa—a young, sharp guy with a snazzy car, only she never introduced him to anybody?'

Dana nodded. 'But he stopped. Too bad for her. She'd have done better going with him than with either Metter or Matt Brent.'

'Would you know *him* if you saw him again?'

'I might.' She smiled. 'You going to take me bowling again?'

'I don't think he bowls. But if he goes where I think he goes, I'll come by for you and we'll go there, too.'

She beamed. 'Tonight?'

'Tonight, tomorrow night. It depends on him.'

'I hope it's tonight.'

'So do I. Now go get dressed. I've got to go to work, and you've got to go home to bed.'

It turned out that tonight *was* the night. I staked out the Manila mansion about seven and settled down for the long wait. Tony Manila didn't go out on dates until late in the evening, but I wanted to make sure I didn't miss him.

Tonight he didn't vary his pattern. It was not quite ten o'clock when his Last-of-the-Convertibles steamed out of the drive and took off toward Shelly's condo. Since I had astutely divined his plans, I was facing in the right direction and took off after him.

146

They went to Hugo's Hideaway again, just as I had figured, and I turned around and drove to Frank's.

It was five after eleven when I entered, and Dana was writhing and jiggling through her last performance under the baby spot. She saw me when I moved in behind the clustered customers at the bar, and I pointed toward the dressing-room door. In another minute, big-breasted Sassie took her place, and Dana hurried back to let me in, without bothering to put her cape on.

As soon as I was inside, she was all over me, just like last night, wrapping her arms around my neck and trying to get me onto the couch. 'I knew you'd come,' she said.

'Yes,' I said and undid her grip. 'But it's business.'

She slid her freed hands over her breasts. 'You want me to identify that man?'

'I want to see if you *can* identify him.'

'I'd do anything for you. You know that.'

'I don't want you to misidentify him just to be agreeable, you know.'

She laughed. 'I know, and I won't. If I've seen him, I'll tell you so.' She unfastened the bottom half of her costume, the string-beaded skirt ensemble, and pushed it down her thighs till it dropped. 'What should I wear?'

'You mean I have a choice?'

She retrieved the costume and dropped it on the couch, then turned to the small rack of dresses and hangers beside the makeup mirror. 'There's the dress I go home in.' She held it up beside her. 'There's my customer dress.' She modelled the black, slinky, taunting number against her body. 'Then there's my party frock.' She showed me a bright, modestly low-cut, full-skirted summer gown. She held it against her bare body and peered down the front of it. 'This is in case rich and handsome young men should invite me to a class party. Are you rich and handsome?'

'Nope. But wear it anyway.'

She slipped it over her head obediently and pulled it down.

'You aren't going to wear anything underneath?'

'What for? The bodice is form-fitted and the skirt is too long to look up.' She paused. 'Do you want me to wear something underneath?'

I said, 'Don't bother. It's a gambling joint, but I don't think they play strip poker.'

Hugo's Hideway, as I may have said before, is a large, low-profile box with a two-storey neon sign and a parking lot the size of O'Hare Airport. Spacious as it was, we still had to drive

148

to the end to leave the car, and Dana decided she should have worn hiking boots instead of heels.

There were three sets of revolving doors at the entrance, with a red-carpeted lobby behind that looked as if it came from a hotel. There were crystal chandeliers, dark panelling, oil paintings, and soaring staircases. The staircases were protected by velvet ropes, and the ropes were protected by pro-football types of the lineman variety. Even through their tuxedos their muscles showed.

The downstairs area behind the lobby was open to the public. It included a nightclub with a band, a restaurant and a cocktail lounge. Anyone could go in, but almost nobody did.

The fun part of the place was up the stairs behind the velvet ropes, but that was for members only, and you had to show your card. This was a private club, the football players told me. It was in accordance with state law, they said. Membership cards could, however, be purchased at the registration desk for a paltry $5 per night or $20 a week, or $150 a year.

There were four men at the registration desk to handle the new-membership traffic. I told the one who waited on me that two one-night memberships would suffice, and he dutifully wrote the names I gave him in the allotted space. I could have called us Popeye the Sailor and Lydia E Pinkham, and he wouldn't have cared. All he wanted was the ten bucks.

I flashed our new cards to the football players, and they unhooked the ropes as if we'd just been crowned and sceptred. 'Have a good evening,' one of them blessed.

Topside, there was a large room humming with games and people. It was craps over there, roulette over here, blackjack yonder, the slot machines along the walls. Here, as in Las Vegas, there were no windows and no clocks. The decor was better, though, and so was the attitude of the people. There was more animation, more noise, more excitement, more interest in the outcome of the next roll of the dice, spin of the wheel, or turn of the card.

The other feature of the upstairs was a large elevator that didn't have a stop on the first floor. This car went to lower regions and, as I'd learned on another occasion, there were many.

Dana and I made an inspection tour of the large upstairs room. Tony Manila and Shelly Polk weren't there. But as we went the route, I could see why. This was the penny-ante room. No wonder there was so much giggling and excitement. The serious, high-stakes side of gambling was taking place somewhere else.

And that would be below stairs.

'This is some place.' Dana said as we completed our circuit. 'I could go for this kind of living.'

I brought her out to the elevator. 'Even up here you can get poor in a hurry. Don't come around unless somebody pays your way.'

Other people were awaiting the elevator, and we boarded the car in a crowd. It was department-store size and needed to be.

Dana and I disembarked at bottom level, two storeys below ground, and here the decor was muted. The floors were tile, the walls two-toned grey, the rooms were smaller, the people quieter and more densely packed.

I looked for the roulette tables first. They were in the biggest room and the most crowded. Blue cigarette smoke hung heavy from the ceiling and stank at ground level. The people moved through it like zombies.

Dana and I stood in the doorway and looked over the crowd. Well, let's say *I* looked over the crowd. Dana didn't know what prey we were after, and she only watched the gaming.

There they were, Tony and Shelly, over in the second bank of roulette tables, their backs to the door. Tony was in tuxedo tonight, and looked like the owner of a yacht. Shelly, was beside him—I saw her profile when she turned to talk to Tony. She was bathed in sequins, and she laid out chips like she was stamping food prices on soup cans in the supermarket. And the chips weren't the five-cent ones they used upstairs. These were worth five dollars each. At these tables you could lose your automobile in half an hour, your house in three.

Tony Manila spotted me at the same time I spotted him. He'd been bent over the board watching Shelly scatter largesse like a farmer sowing seed, and it was only the thick wavy blackness of his hair and the cut of the shoulders that caught my attention. That's when he looked up and glanced quickly over his shoulder, and his gleaming eyes settled on Dana and me. They went blank, like the eyes of a shark, and he whispered to Shelly, then came for us fast around the end of the table, through the crowds.

I gripped Dana and pointed. 'There. That one. Moving there. See? Coming our way.'

She saw, all right, and she clutched my arm. 'It's him.' She pulled on me, suddenly frightened. 'Let's get out of here.'

I held her fast. I'm not brave. I just wanted her to think I was. 'He's not going to hurt you.' I said. 'You're sure he's the one?'

'Yes. He went with Nerissa first. He's the one.' She pulled again. 'Please. Let's go.'

I released her. 'You go. I have business.'

She slipped behind me, but stayed, holding me with both hands, peering out around me.

Tony came up to me as close as he dared, ignoring the girl, trying to back me off with his presence. We almost bumped, but I didn't retreat. I'd placed my back against the door frame.

'You thick-skulled guys don't learn very fast, do you?' he said. 'I was too easy on you. When I told you to stay away from me, you shoulda listened.'

I said, 'My mistake. I thought you told me to stay away from your *girl*. By the way, have you met my friend?' I tried to pull Dana into better view.

He ignored her. 'You blew it, buster,' he told me. 'You had your chance.'

I kept trying. 'My friend here says you used to go with Nerissa Claire. How *is* Nerissa these days?'

He wanted to kill me on the spot, but he didn't quite dare. In the first place, he knew I carried a gun—he'd have searched me after he smashed my skull. (Because I'd been left intact didn't mean I hadn't been combed.) And he knew what I could do in a fight. And a room full of witnesses wouldn't be a good scene for an execution.

So he measured me, took in the crowd, thought about his gun and my gun, and decided to postpone my death till a more convenient time arose.

But there was no doubt he intended to kill me. For one thing his flush disappeared, his anger lessened, and he became coherent. 'I'm gonna give you three to disappear,' he said. 'And I mean, for keeps. You understand me, buster?'

'Where's Nerissa?' I said. 'What've you done with her?'

He studied me, his fists clenching and unclenching. I could see him contemplating the cost of my burial.

'Come on,' I said. 'There's no need to get sore. Just tell me where Nerissa is, and I won't bother you any more.'

He shook his head. 'You got the wrong guy, buster. I don't know any Nerissa. Take off.'

I indicated what of Dana was visible. 'My friend here says you used to date her.'

'So what? I haven't seen her since last October.'

'How'd you meet her roommate, Shelly, then?'

He said to me, 'Next time you see your friends, tell them goodbye.' Then he turned on his heel and went away.

Dana pulled me out into the hall. She was shaking. 'Stay away from him,' she said. 'You shouldn't have gone near him. Can't you tell he's dangerous?'

'I can tell,' I said. 'Nerissa made some nice friends.'

'He scared me, even back then. He had a lot of money but a cruel face.'

'No wonder Nerissa didn't introduce him around.'

'No wonder she ditched him so fast.'

'Yeah?' I stroked my chin. 'Maybe she didn't ditch him at all? He might have ditched her, but I don't think anybody ever ditched *him*.'

Dana held my arm. 'Listen, can we go now? That was what you wanted me for, wasn't it?'

I nodded. 'But I didn't find out all I wanted. He didn't answer all my questions.'

Dana pulled my arm in the direction of the elevator. 'He doesn't know anything,' she insisted. 'He hasn't shown up at Frank's since last October, like he said. Nerissa was going with Matt Brent. There wasn't any other man in her life! I'm telling you, Matt wouldn't have stood for it.'

'Sure, sure.' I soothed. 'Except that the girl he's with tonight he picked up at Nerissa's apartment. He knows more than he's saying—a

155

hell of a lot more.' I patted her arm. 'Come on, let's place a few bets at Tony's table. Maybe I can get to know him better.'

We didn't gamble after all. I circled the room twice, leading Dana by the hand, but Tony and Shelly weren't there. They'd disappeared through another exit. And after all his threats? What was he running away for?

I took Dana home, doing the routine manoeuvres to make sure Tony couldn't ambush or follow me. I mean, I suspected he left the casino for reasons other than fear.

I kissed her good night on the doorstep, and she tried to get me to come up. She wanted another night together on her cramped couch. I said no, I was going to get some sleep.

'Here you'll be safe. Tony doesn't know where I live.'

'The answer is still no. I need some sleep.'

'I'll let you sleep,' she said. 'I'll even sleep on the floor.'

As I say, with girls it's never just fun and games. Hidden behind every one-night stand lies a two-night stand, then a three-nighter, and the next thing you know, it's 'Where the hell have you been?' and 'What are you trying to do, run out on me?' Women have beautiful bodies. I love them. But their bodies come with chains.

So I resisted, and for once it didn't take all that much willpower. It had been a tough day, and my battered head and body were rebelling. I really wasn't in the mood for sex, and sex was what she was peddling no matter how much she talked about sleep.

She gave up at last and kissed me and warned me to be careful—Tony might be waiting. I said I would, and I was. But there was no sign of Tony.

CHAPTER SEVENTEEN

What wakened me was someone yelling and banging on my condo door. It was pitch black, and the red numbers on my digital clock radio said 3:33. A helluva lot of sleep I was getting. I hadn't been in bed an hour and a half. I switched on the light and put my feet on the floor. It sounded as if someone was hollering 'Police!' From the banging, it sounded like cops.

I got up, slipped into a dressing gown, put my feet into slippers, and took my .38 out of the bureau drawer. I carried it in my right hand into the guest room, which has a window out back. In there, red and yellow lights swept across the ceiling, and outside were three real police cars with all their beacon lights going. It *was* the police—the police and some gawking neighbours.

I went down to the front door, throwing on lights *en route,* turned the keys and kept the chain lock on. Detective Sergeant Lasky and two patrolmen were on the storm porch. I don't know why it's always Lasky!

'Shush,' I said, 'you'll wake the baby. What the hell do you want?'

'Open up. Police.'

I pocketed the gun, opened up, and Lasky, with the two patrolmen at his heels, bulled through like a psuedo All-American. The two patrolmen were young—after my time—and they viewed me with glittering suspicion...the Lasky kind. I should maintain better contact with the P.D, consort with the newcomers, build contacts. Lasky I can't do anything about, but neither can anybody else from what I hear.

We went into the kitchen where the brightest lights were. Lasky told me to sit, and I told him what he could do. There's a mean streak in him, and this brought it out. 'You're riding for a fall, mister, and I'm gonna be there when you take it. And I'm gonna ask you a question. Do you think I'd help you up?'

I said, 'I think you'd kick my head in. Why should you treat me special?'

He hauled back as if to swing, but he knew better. The patrolmen leaped in to stop him, but that only made it look good. He wouldn't have hit me on the worst day he ever knew. It wasn't that he was afraid of me, it was what would happen to his career.

Lasky straightened up and brushed himself off, scowling as if I'd had a narrow escape. 'Where've you been tonight?' he asked, paying attention to his rehabilitation.

'Who wants to know? Besides you?'

Now he faced me, hands on hips. 'Is that your answer? You want to call a lawyer? You don't want to answer my questions without a lawyer present?'

'That depends on what you're accusing me of doing. I happen to have been asleep.'

'For how long?'

'An hour and a half. It would've been longer if you hadn't come.'

Lasky said over his shoulder. 'Get that!' and one of the patrolmen scribbled in his notebook.

'I don't want to wake up my lawyer unless it's really necessary,' I said. 'Can you give me a clue as to what crime I've committed?'

'You can't guess, can you?'

'That's right.'

'Where have you been tonight?'

'What time tonight?'

'The whole time. From eight o'clock on.'

'Working.'

'At what?'

'My job. What do you think I work at?'

'Who was the broad you were with?'

'What broad?'

'You were seen tonight with a broad.'

That was interesting. 'Says who?'

'Stop stalling. You were with a broad to-night. I've got two witnesses who can identify her. So knock off being so smart ass. What's her name?'

'Ask your informants.'

'I'm asking you.'

'It's none of your damned business.'

'I'm making it my business. Either you answer or you wake up your lawyer.'

I said, testily, 'I was working at my job, and the nature of my job and the name of the client who hires me are privileged information. You call my lawyer if you don't think I know what I'm talking about.'

'Would her name, perhaps, be Dana Doxey?'

I laughed harshly. 'Who's your stoolie, Jake Metter?'

'It's interesting that you should ask.'

'It sure as hell is. Where does he fit in?'

Lasky smiled with ghoulish delight. 'Jake Metter happens to be assigned to this case.'

'What case is that?'

'A case of murder—as if you didn't know.'

I felt a sudden, relentless pang. 'Murder? Who got killed?'

That brought forth a more fiendish grin. 'You look pale, Kaye. You look unnerved. You look like you need to lie down. You want to lie down, Kaye? We can go down into your nice living room, and you can lie on the couch and tell us about it. How'd that suit you? Get it off your chest. You'll feel better.'

I grabbed him and pulled him up close. *'Who got killed?'*

The two cops jumped me. I got the stick-end of a billy in the gut, and a forearm around my throat, cutting off my wind. Then I was on the floor against the wall with my senses reeling. Three behemoths were standing over me, spinning around and around.

Lasky gave me a stiff boot in the ribs. He wanted to get in on the fun. 'The sonuvabitch,' he growled. 'He needs a working over.'

They dragged me up into a kitchen chair. Lasky bent close. 'Where'd you and Dana go tonight?'

'Is she the one who's dead?'

'What do you think we're doing here? You been out with anybody else tonight?'

There was a lump of lead the size of a football in my stomach. If I'd stayed with her... If I hadn't been so damned skittish. You don't have to run away from women just because they get a look in their eye. You can make the rules: you don't have to go by theirs. Dana was dead, and I'd only just left her. I looked up at Lasky, and I wasn't thinking straight. I said, 'Who did it?'

'That's what we're asking you.'

'How was she killed?'

His eyes gleamed. 'Why don't you tell us?'

If I hadn't been so shook up, I'd have known that was a dumb question. I tried to ask one that might get me some information. 'Why do you think I did it?'

'You were the last one to see her alive. That a good reason?'

'Who says so?' (I was wondering who the hell had seen us together, besides Tony and Shelly.)

'How about a guy named Jerry Nemo?'

'Who the hell is Jerry Nemo? I never heard of him.'

'He tends bar at Frank's go-go saloon. You know about Frank's don't you? You going to deny you hang out at Frank's?'

'How does the bartender at Frank's do a make on me? What've you been doing to him? He doesn't know my name.'

'He knows your face. You want me to put you in a lineup and let him pick out the guy who was hustling Dana?'

I ached for Dana, but I was beginning to function. Some glimmers of intelligence were filtering through. Jerry might have described me to the cops, but he didn't know me. And Lasky wouldn't decide from the description that only Simon Kaye could fit it.

But Jake Metter was on the case. Jake not only knew Dana, he knew *I* knew her. And if he was with Lasky at the scene, he'd know who the victim was. Thereafter, it would be easy for them to decide Jerry's description fitted me.

I didn't answer Lasky's question. I said, instead, 'You told me Metter's on the case. Where is he? Why isn't he in here too?'

'He's here. He's outside.'

'Well, then, you bring the chicken-livered sonuvabitch in here. He's the one who put the finger on me. Get him in here and we'll talk!'

Lasky played innocent. 'He didn't finger you. He doesn't know you know Dana. He just happens to be on the case.'

'Sure he just happens to be on the case. And you go to an apartment and you find a body.

And it turns out that Metter recognizes it. And don't give me that crap that he doesn't know I knew her. He saw me with her at a bowling alley two nights ago. He knows I knew her all right. And he tells you I know her, and that's all you need. You talk to Jerry and decide I'm the guy he saw leaving the bar with Dana tonight. Or maybe he doesn't remember seeing me go out with her. Maybe all you did was tell Jerry I'm the guy you want to fry and he went along. There'd be a lot of people who'd close a trap on me because I had an in with the girl they leched for.'

Lasky said, 'You're talking cockeyed. You need a psychiatrist.'

'Psychiatrist? A year ago you couldn't pronounce the word. Now it's the carpet you sweep the dirt under. Metter told you I was with Dana at a bowling alley. Don't bother to deny it. It's the only way you could come around here blaming me for her murder. So, did you ask the sonuvabitch *why* I took Dana to the bowling alley? Did he tell you she wasn't in bowling clothes?'

'I don't know anything about any bowling alley.'

'Jake's clamming up on you, Lasky. He forgot to tell you he's the one who introduced Matt Brent to the broad his wife killed him over.'

164

'What's that got to do with tonight's murder?'

'Dana could identify him, and he didn't want her pointing her finger at him. That's what I took her to see him at the bowling alley for, and that's why he's after my scalp. I'll tell you what, Lasky. Bring Metter in here and we'll go down into my living room and let's all talk about Dana Doxey. You might learn something.'

Lasky wasn't letting me derail him. 'I'll bring Metter in when I want to bring him in,' he told me. 'Right now it's just going to be you and me.'

'Are you accusing me of murdering Dana Doxey? Is that your angle?'

He leered. 'Actually, I'm not accusing you of a blessed thing.' ('Blessed' wasn't really the word he used, but let's not be crude). He gestured magnanimously. 'But don't let me stop you from calling your lawyer.'

I was running this scene through my think tank, trying to make things add up. Lasky was really pushing me. But what did he have to work with? He'd talked to the bartender at Frank's. The bartender could testify that I went off with Dana for three-quarters of an hour two evenings ago, he could testify that I left with Dana when she finished work tonight. Okay, that's enough connection to rate Lasky's interrogation, but not enough to rate his threats. He must have another witness fingering me. Maybe there was a neighbour who saw me bring her home?

Except that I left her at her door, so that couldn't be the answer.

I thought of Lemon Eyes. Maybe he'd been watching the building and claimed not only that I saw her home, but that I also went in with her—and didn't come out till...whenever? It could be Lemon Eyes's idea of revenge.

The one thing I was sure of was that Lasky had something up his sleeve. It wasn't enough to arrest me for, so he was using it to lay a trap. And the moment I lied to him, I'd spring the trap. He, like Metter, wanted me hanged, but it couldn't be done with the evidence at hand. He was trying to get me to help him tie the rope. And Lasky, thick as he might be, unpleasant as he might be, knew the sharp edges of the law, knew where they could bite and where they could be bitten. He saw me as a live suspect, not because he hated my guts, but because he thought he had a case.

'I don't need a lawyer,' I said, 'because you don't have anything on me. I don't know what you're doing here.'

He said belligerently, 'I'll tell you what I'm doing here. I'm asking you where you went with the Doxey doll when you picked her up after work five hours ago. I want a blow-by-blow account.' He smirked. 'I wantta know how you single guys make out.'

'Forget it,' I said. 'You wouldn't believe it.'

'Try me.'

It was a waste of time, but I wanted it on the record. 'She's been assisting me on an investigation. She's been identifying people who're connected with the go-go dancer Matt Brent got killed over.'

'Oh?' Lasky sneered. 'She's your assistant? She's a pretty damned beautiful assistant. I should have assistants like her.' He winked at his men. 'You know something, Kaye? In her apartment, on her bureau, is this colour photograph of her in the nude. She's posing stark naked. And you want to know something else? She's got a helluva beautiful body.'

'She did have, but she put on weight.'

'You've seen the picture, huh? You like the picture?'

I didn't know how much he knew, but I knew better than to lie. This was more of that bait he was trying to trap me with. 'Yes,' I said. 'She showed it to me.'

'It must have driven you bananas. What happened, Kaye? Did she reject your advances?

I mean, you think you're a pretty handsome stud. I mean, you think all the girls go ga-ga over your muscles and your physique...'

I was getting pretty tense. I said, 'Watch it, fat boy.'

He didn't like that. He wasn't all that fat, but fat enough to turn red. 'Tell me what she's like naked, you handsome stud,' he said. 'Tell me what you did to her when she told you to get lost.' He goaded me further. 'You couldn't take a turndown, could you? Tell me about it. Tell me what it felt like to get turned down by a beautiful broad like Dana Doxey.'

I cooled it. I said, 'Actually, we were going to get married.'

That narrowed his eyes. I wouldn't play his game, and now it was his turn to steam. 'She's a go-go dancer,' he snarled. 'You single guys, you'll go after anything!'

I came out of my seat and whacked him with a backhand karate chop The two cops with him hit me with their billies, and it was half an hour before we got under way again. Lasky was warning me that one more act like that and he'd have me on assault of a police officer, and I was mumbling that it was justifiable and I had witnesses.

We went around the mulberry bush again, but I don't think his heart was in it. The side of his face was black and blue from where I'd hit him, and it was swollen enough to half close one eye. He would have looked funny, but this wasn't a funny kind of night. That side of his mouth was swollen too, and the lips didn't move much. He pretended there was nothing wrong with him, but his words were muffled, and it would have to be a helluva big door he'd need to say he walked into. Never mind, I looked worse than he did, and I felt at least as bad. I didn't have much heart either.

'I'm gonna tell you what I think,' he muttered. 'You picked up Dana Doxey at eleven o'clock this morning, only she wasn't assisting you in anything. She was dating you. She thought you were a big deal. You'd taken her out before. You were making a play for her.

'And tonight you got to take her home. And tonight she showed you that pretty picture she's got of herself on her bureau—where she's stark naked. And it gave you ideas. Except she didn't like your ideas.' He gave me his measured look. 'How does it sound so far?'

'I've got a better story,' I sighed. 'I picked her up at eleven, took her out for a hamburger and a glass of beer and dropped her on her doorstep at half-past one and that was that.'

'Is that what you're gonna claim? Is that what you're gonna tell the D.A?'

The thought of Lemon Eyes and his switch-blade crossed my mind. 'That's my story,' I said. 'I couldn't get to first base. She closed the door in my face and went upstairs.' Then I said, 'And somebody was waiting for her up there and stabbed her to death. Do you think the D.A will quarrel with that one?'

An unchaste gleam came into Lasky's eyes. 'That's a pretty good story for an amateur. How many times did this intruder stab her?'

'Let's see,' I said. 'Three times. Right?'

Lasky grinned. He was forgetting his swollen face. 'Maybe you overlooked one.'

'That's strange,' I said. 'I only remember three.'

He knew then I was making fun of him. He looked me over with some ill-concealed hate. 'I'm gonna leave you for now,' he said, and pointed a threatening finger. 'But don't think you're clear. You killed that dame, and you're gonna fry for it.'

He beckoned to the two big cops who'd worked me over and turned on his heel.

Doors closed, footsteps retreated down the outside stairs, engines started, and cars drove away. I was left battered, beaten, sick, and— at last—alone.

CHAPTER EIGHTEEN

It was only when the quiet settled in and all sound had stopped that it really hit me. Dana was dead. I'd seen her a few hours ago, and if I'd stayed with her, she'd almost certainly still be alive.

I brewed myself a pot of coffee and smoked cigarettes. There was no point in trying to go back to sleep. Of course, there wasn't much point in staying awake unless I did more than stew and fret and berate myself.

My body ached from the new beating, and I had to walk around to stem the pain. My face was untouched. Those cops hadn't hit me on the head. They'd given it to me in the body, where it didn't show and where it hurt the most.

So I paced and took aspirin and tried to make my brain function. I keep the aspirin people in business. I think they invented the stuff just for me.

As best I could put it together, somebody had reported Dana dead. Lasky and Metter had gone to the scene. She'd been killed with a knife, stabbed four times. I could guess the rest. They'd questioned the neighbours, they'd woken up Ben Schill. That had led them to Jerry Nemo and, with Metter's help, on to me.

And they came at me, leaning hard. Granted, Lasky likes to flex his muscles, and Jake Metter did want to see me in thumb screws, but there were other reasons behind their act. For one thing, they had to have something more pointing to me than a bartender's description. For another, if they chased me so hard, it meant there was nobody else. They had no other suspects.

So who did it? I went through the list.

It could be Lemon Eyes. If he thought she'd been sullied, he might have wanted to 'purify' her.

If sex were the motive, it could be Ben Schill: she wasn't putting out for him and he was the resentful type.

It could be any one of the ogling customers who drooled in their beers when she shimmied on the stand. They could have followed her home the way Lemon Eyes did.

If she had damaging information, it could be Tony Manila. She claimed he didn't know where she lived, but he'd find out fast enough if he wanted her.

It wasn't much of a list. There weren't many people who'd like her dead. And it wasn't my business anyway. Murders are for the cops to solve, and once they got themselves untracked, they'd get on with it. In due time they'd come up with the killer—despite the headlines, they usually do—and there was no reason for me to butt my nose in.

But I was going to do some butting anyway. And I don't mean because Lasky wouldn't like it, but because Dana would. If I could help nail her killer, I'd be lighting a candle to her memory.

I stopped pacing and aching when the sun melted the early clouds. It was six o'clock and already the day promised to be a scorcher. Lemon Eyes was the first guy to see. He had a penchant for knives, and Dana had been stabbed.

I got to his pad at quarter of seven. The workaday crowd hadn't yet hit the streets, and things were quiet. The address was a slummy apartment, the kind whose landlords don't answer the phone, where the faucets leak, the cockroaches intimidate the rats and the radiators lie dead in the winter.

The mailbox for Richard Loomis gave the

room number as 11, and I pushed through the inside door to the interior hall. There were no locks.

Room 11 was front left, away from the staircase, and I was polite. I knocked before using my passkey.

There was no problem getting in. The chain lock wasn't in place, and the reason was that Lemon Eyes wasn't there. I hadn't thought he would be.

The bed hadn't been slept in either. It was against the wall and neatly made up. The rest of the room was neat, too, but that's the last thing you'd notice.

I have to tell you about that room. It was all pictures. And every one was of Dana. On the wall beside the door was a large Frank's Bar poster he must have swiped from the vestibule, which described the luscious, beautiful exotic dancers who performed inside. In the centre was a fuzzy blow-up of what probably was some homecoming queen, scantily but properly attired in spangles and crown. In insets were portrait pictures of the three girls who did the performing inside—Dana was one, Lucille was another, and Nerissa, presumably, was the third. Dana's picture was untouched, but the other two had thick black crosses painted across their faces, so deliber-

174

ately obliterating the features that the only way I could be sure of Lucille was her hairline.

Everywhere else were pictures, snapshots, enlargements from snapshots, taken under all conditions but mostly in the wrong light and the wrong direction—Dana from the rear, walking from work at night; Dana fitting her key in the door at the top of the apartment steps under the light; Dana coming down the apartment steps in bright sunshine.

The *pièce de résistance* was something. It was a picture of Dana on stage doing her dance, snapped by Lemon Eyes using fast colour film. He'd had it blown up to larger than life, a six-foot blurry Dana, wearing her bead-string skirt, her bare feet hidden by the scalloped line of customers' pates, her arms out, her head half turned. It wouldn't have been a bad picture as a five-by-seven—not great, but pretty good. Lemon Eyes had it fastened to the inside of the door, facing the bed, directly opposite his pillow. It was his pride and joy. The thing about it, though, was that he had pasted black tape over her nipples. Don't ask me what that was supposed to mean. All I know is it takes all kinds, and when it comes to kinds, he was in a class by himself.

I did a rough search while I was there to see if he had any information of value: notes on scrap papers, a Klu Klux Klan hood under his mattress, a Kremlin code book in his shaving kit, or maybe his suitcase missing and his bureau drawers empty. I didn't come up with anything. There was no suitcase, but there were some clothes. He could have packed a bag and left; he could just as well not have owned a bag and the clothes were all he had.

I closed shop, making sure Lemon Eyes, if he returned, wouldn't know his shrine had been violated. Outside, a stout old man sat on the steps in the sun and played with his cane. I asked him where he thought Richard Loomis might be, and he shook his head. Nobody knew when Mr Loomis came or went. Richard Loomis didn't keep other people's hours.

'Know where he works?'

'He don't work—leastways at anything that has regular hours.'

'Where does he get his money?'

'I didn't know he had any.'

'He must eat.'

'He must sleep, too, but I never seen him do neither.'

In other words, Pops didn't know anything. According to him, neither did anybody else.

CHAPTER NINETEEN

I spent a routine morning at the office, but I wasn't feeling routine. Even Eileen noticed it. I shouldn't say 'even,' because Eileen notices everything. You walk in one pound overweight and she'll omit the cream or sugar on your coffee break. 'I thought you'd be dieting,' she'll say. Today she flashed a bright smile when she brought in the coffee and said, 'Want to break down and have a slug of brandy in it?'

When I looked at her she said, 'Good for what ails you,' and kept the phony smile on high beam.

She thinks she's got me figured—well, I've got *her* figured too. And I let her know it. 'It's a working day, Miss Nightingale, and the sun's far from the yardarm.'

She let go of the smile. 'But you aren't doing much work. You're living in the past. The recent past. Something's happened, hasn't it? Just last night?'

'I'd just as soon not talk about it.'

She gave a wistful smile. 'I wasn't suggesting

therapy, I was suggesting brandy.'

I let her give me a slug.

It didn't do me any good. I couldn't get Dana out of my mind any more than I could get the pain out of my body.

At eleven o'clock Leonard Wood phoned, as any anxious client will phone when I haven't reported to him in the time span he thinks is his own. Where was Nerissa Claire, he wanted to know.

I was trying to find out, I explained.

'And what luck are you having?'

'So far, not a great deal.'

'So,' Leonard said, 'what am *I* supposed to do?'

'Be patient. The messages I'm getting are that this was a planned disappearance, not an unlucky accident—meaning, she didn't happen to decide to elope just when Carla Brent was killing her husband. She had decided to leave the scene for another reason.'

'Like what?'

'If I could answer that, I could put my hands on her. You have to understand one thing, Mr Wood. A detective is not a clairvoyant.'

He didn't like having to retreat without information, especially when I said I was going to need more money. I sensed he was tempted to vent his opinion of my detective ability and pull the plug on further funds. In fact, that was what I was *hoping* he'd do. The hell with the whole thing.

Unfortunately for Mr Wood—and for me too—he didn't have other alternatives. He said he wanted me to continue on the case.

'How long,' he asked, acrimoniously, 'do you suppose I'm going to have to wait to get a positive reply from you?'

'Monday morning at ten o'clock.' (There was nothing magic about that moment, but I had to say something.)

'You'll hear from me then,' he said. 'And what you have for me better be *good*.' (He made it sound like Life and Death but all a failure would cost me was those further funds.)

Eileen went to lunch at noon, and I was still fidgeting, wondering why I was so possessed about Dana's death. To feel responsible because I wasn't there to protect her is sick. I might rue the fact, but I'm not going to feel guilty about it.

Was it because she was young and beautiful? Because I'd slept with her? Nonsense.

Was it because it got me off the hook? Was I secretly relieved that I was free of her clutching arms and was suffering pangs of guilt? Jack McGuire, my priest friend, would love that one. He knows I have no more truck with Freud than I do with God.

But something sure as hell was bugging me, and it wasn't my aches and pains. About the time Eileen got back from lunch, a glimmer broke through. Who the hell was Dana Doxey anyway? Where did she come from? To whom did she belong?

I had Eileen get me the records room at the morgue. I know one of the girls there, though I almost wish I didn't. Her name is Muriel, and she has the face and figure to play the lead in caveman epics where fetching lasses in skimpy loinclothes and skimpier tops run over the rocks, throw spears and wrestle gorillas. The trouble is, her mind is on the same track as her body, and it's hell trying to talk business to her. I said I wanted the vital statistics on a murder victim brought in earlier this morning, a girl by the name of Dana Doxey.

'Vital statistics of a broad, huh? What're you trying to do, make me jealous?'

She was only kidding, of course. Only Muriel can kid like that.

I said it was really important, and she said, 'You're a little late, you know. She's dead.' Muriel was being a real bitch today. I hadn't seen her in a couple of seasons, and she was letting me know where I stood.

180

I won't go into the rest of the conversation, for it was as inane as the above. After a lot of manoeuvring and a couple of semi-promises, I did wheedle out of her what I wanted. Dana's height and weight weren't on file, Muriel told me, for she hadn't been measured yet. 'She's got a nice figure, though: bust thirteen, waist thirty-three, hips forty-eight. It says here on the sheet that she's fifty years old.'

That was how she relayed the physical reportage, which didn't matter. What I wanted was: name and address of next of kin, who she was, and where she was from.

They didn't have that. Muriel swore up and down she wasn't teasing me, that the whole sheet on Dana Doxey was blank except for name and present address. 'Why don't you call the police?' she suggested, even trying to be helpful.

'That's an idea,' I answered politely. With Lasky in charge, I'd need an order from the mayor to get a hello. And I doubted the police would know any more than the morgue did. One would brief the other.

I thanked Muriel for her help, and she said, 'How about getting interested in a live girl for a change? I'm free after five.'

With her looks, she doesn't need to beg. Maybe that explains why she's hard up for dates, but, as I say, Freud can do the explaining. It's not my department.

At half-past one, I left the office, giving Frank's Bar as my destination. Eileen wrinkled her nose. 'Isn't that where girls dance without their clothes on?'

'They wear a little something, so I've been told.'

'So you've been told? Meaning you want me to believe you don't already know?'

'This is business. It's really business.'

She shook her head. 'I simply don't understand men.'

I stared at her cleavage long enough to make her blush—and that takes some doing. I said, 'I think you understand men better than any girl I ever knew.'

We parted and I didn't look back. I didn't dare.

It was blistering in Frank's Bar. For one thing, the sun was high, and the painted windows were facing it. For another, there was no air conditioning. They'd turn that on at three o'clock when the girls began to dance. (Ben Schill also didn't want sweat dripping off their nipples.)

Jerry Nemo, the poor man's Tony Galento, was behind the bar with two customers to serve, and he was the only one of the three who wasn't sweating. (He not only moved slowly, but he also had a fan blowing on him from under the counter.) Jerry was the one who'd fingered me to the cops last night, and he gave me a double take and braced himself when I came in. Maybe he thought I was in jail. Maybe he thought I was going to chop out his liver.

I gave him a steel eye and put an elbow on the bar. 'The cops give you a hard time last night?'

He grunted. It could have meant yes, no or maybe.

'Ben Schill in his office?'

Ben was bigger and grosser than Jerry. Jerry grunted in the affirmative. Ben would take care of me.

I went back there and found three listless young girls standing outside his office trying to get as much air as they could through the open back door to the alley. They were motionless and gathered where the circulation was trying to keep their frocks from wilting. They stared at Ben's door as if it were sacred and ogled me with envy when I rapped on it and walked in.

Ben was behind his desk, poring over some papers. There was a floor fan in a corner blowing towards the open window. There were also three unpleasant male members of our species lounging on chairs beside him. All they made me think of was pigs in a pen.

Ben looked up in sharp irritation. He thought I was one of the waiting girls. Then he beamed with recognition and rose to hold out his ham of a hand. 'You came at just the right time,' he said and waved to a chair. 'Join our party. This here is Frank Geno—he's the major stockholder in Frank's Bar. This here's Al Stultz, another large stockholder. This is Manny Abel—he's cook in the restaurant next door and a great judge of horseflesh, if you know what I mean.'

I said, 'Well, thanks and all that, Ben, but I've only got a minute. Could I see your employment application for Dana?'

I could hear muted gasps from the others present. I had mentioned the unmentionable. Dana no longer existed.

Ben still caressed my sleeve, coaxing me into a chair. God, he was a big man—and he wasn't even trying. 'Yeah, what a crying shame,' he said. 'She was a great pal, Dana was. I don't know who coulda done such a thing. The cops had me up half the night pumping me about her. You involved in the case?'

'I'm trying to track down her background. If you know—'

'Me? I don't know from nothing. It'd be on her application sheet.'

'Well, if you'd just let me see it...'

'Sure,' he said. 'We can get to that later. First I'd like to have you present for our party. Another judge would be a good thing.'

It was going to be quid pro quo then. I said, 'Her sheet first, *then* the party.'

Ben didn't argue, not in front of his high-powered clientele. He got me the sheet and he smiled when he gave it to me, but he couldn't help muttering that it was rude to read in public.

I pretended I didn't hear him and sat in a vacant chair between him and next door's cook. The cook smelled of fish—last Friday's fish.

The sheet was the same as the one I'd seen for Nerissa. I was afraid that, like Nerissa, Dana had left the background questions blank. On the contrary, she'd filled in the whole page. That was hopeful, and I got out my notebook to copy down the info. It was data that the police should have picked up and relayed to the morgue for their files. So far the morgue didn't have it, so where was the goof? It didn't matter. I copied the material for myself.

I was halfway through when Ben Schill put

aside a sheaf of similar sheets and said, 'Let's have Jean Smith!' He chuckled and repeated the name: 'Jean Smith. Pretty original, huh? Twenty years old. Black hair. Five-feet-five. Thirty-four, twenty-two, thirty-four. Anybody who wants to check that for accuracy, the tape is right here.' Ben Schill proudly clapped a hand on a tape reel that could have measured the Empire State Building.

I looked up from my scribbles as the first girl came in. She had black hair, as advertised, and the dimensions looked right. But she wasn't twenty, not by the most charitable guess. I don't think she was even pushing eighteen.

She was trying to look old enough, and she wore makeup to help, but the really young kids can't put it across. It's the way they behave. Watch them and see. A gal opts for a go-go dancer's position, it's raw sex. It's not beauty, artistic talent, communing with the gods, or 'just another way to make a living.' It's raw sex. And the purveyors of raw sex, like the purveyors of milk formula or diet pills or toilet tissue, are going to lay their careers on the line making you believe that their product, be it raw sex or toilet tissue, is what makes the world go around.

So the twenty-year-old has learned this, if she's smart, has sensed it if she isn't. And she sharpens her claws on the appropriate bias. The kids—the sixteen- to eighteen-year-olds—haven't caught on yet. They still believe in ethics and ideals.

So in came this dark-haired child trying to look mature, hoping Ben Schill and his three cronies wouldn't question her age—as if they cared. Their measurement of talent was by the cupful, meaning A, B, C, or D. As for me, I worked at finishing my copying.

The girl nodded obediently in response to Ben's admonitions. She looked frightened.

'Turn around,' Ben said, making a circle with a finger. 'Give us a three-sixty. Backsides are important too. Girls aren't all front. Only ninety percent front.' He laughed at his joke, and the others joined in. The girl didn't. She did a slow, careful turn, looking behind her as she went, seeking approbation. All she got was ogling.

When she was full front again, Ben gave her his frightening grin. 'Okay honey. So far, so good. Now let's see what you look like without the dress.'

She swallowed, reached behind for a zipper, then grasped the dress around the hips, cross-handed, and drew it up.

'Hold it,' Ben interrupted before she'd half started. 'Do it slow-like. You aren't getting ready for bed, you know. You're stripping for us men. Make us hungry. Make us want you.'

She did it more slowly, but that was all. She didn't know how to be sexy, only natural. That's what I mean about age. It would come to her in time. The skirt rose to her waist, then she paused to pull down and adjust the white half-slip underneath. Ben said irritably, 'Christ, what do you think you're doing?'

She swallowed and resumed raising the dress, up past the band of her slip, up over her white-bra'd breasts, up to her neck.

When she tried to pull the dress over her head, Ben told her to stop. 'Just stay like that and let us look at you,' he ordered, leaving her with her face covered, the rest of her fetchingly revealed in her undergarments. Ben believed in milking his interviews. 'Yeah,' he said appreciatively. 'Not bad.' His companions drooled and nodded vigorously.

'Okay, continue,' he said, and the girl, blind with the dress over her face, pulled it the rest of the way off and shuddered with relief at being able to see again. In that company it was terrifying to be blindfolded and exposed.

'Okay, cutie,' Ben said when she draped the dress carefully over a spare chair, 'now let's see your tits.'

That, of course, was what it was all about—

what she'd come there for—and she handled herself with more aplomb. She reached behind, undid the bra without a mis-cue, and slipped it down her arms to one hand. This was where she felt she had what it took, and she was right. She got whistles from the crew, and even Ben's eyes gleamed. 'Yeah,' he said admiringly, and you could tell he was already dreaming of getting his hands on them. She might think they were only to look at, but she was new in the game.

Ben had her turn this way and that, do a complete about, show herself from the back and the sides. This, you could tell, she didn't mind doing. It might be her first time, but this was the act she wanted to pursue, and she had to believe in herself. She even smiled in the glow of their admiration. What an easy way to get a job!

She thought, when Ben had had sufficient, that it was back into her dress and sign a contract. None of the other girls outside could match her development.

It wasn't quite like that. Ben didn't say, 'Get dressed.' He said, 'now take off that stupid slip.'

She looked at him in surprise.

'The slip. The slip!' He gestured. 'Get rid of it.'

'But why?'

'I wanta see your legs, for Chrissake. Show me your legs! What're ya trying to hide your legs for?'

'Well, I wasn't trying to hide them.' She flushed red, then reluctantly hooked her thumbs in the waistband and pulled the thing down, stepping out of it and laying it with her bra and dress. Now she was wearing a pair of white underpants, and her limbs and otherwise bare body were all anyone could ask for, but the flush wouldn't leave her face. Showing her underpants hadn't been part of her preparation, and it took adjustment, especially with the concentration of eyes on that part of her.

'Perk up,' Ben told her, making her turn around. 'You got nothing to be ashamed of.'

She went through her paces as ordered and waited for the end. Then Ben said, 'Okay, not bad. Now let's see you without the pants.'

'Now wait a second,' she erupted with a sudden burst of spunk.

'What's the matter with you?' he snapped back. 'You one of those modest broads? You got a hang-up or something?'

'I showed you my legs,' young Miss Smith said testily. 'I showed you everything else.'

'Not everything.'

'Everything I need to show you. This is a

topless bar. You're hiring girls to dance topless...not bottomless.'

'Not yet it's bottomless, but we're gonna get a licence any day now, and when we do, all you girls are gonna go bottomless. And you gotta be ready.'

'Well, when that happens, I'll think about it.'

'When that happens ain't gonna be when you think about it. You think about it now or you don't get hired. Either a girl does it or she doesn't. I don't want anybody who doesn't. You got two choices, sister. Either you take off your pants and show us guys here everything you've got, or pick up your things and tell the next girl to come in.'

He gave her two seconds and snapped his fingers. 'Come on, come on. Which is it?'

She was almost in tears. 'Please. I'm trying.'

Ben said to the others, 'What do you say? We throw her out?'

'Please wait. I'll do it,' she said, and now the tears were starting down her cheeks. 'I just have to get used to... Just let me get used to it.'

'Whaddaya think, we got all afternoon?'

She hooked her thumbs in the band of her pants. 'I'll do it. I said I'll do it.' She wiped her cheeks with one hand and hooked her thumb again.

I stood up and chucked Dana Doxey's application form onto Ben's desk. 'Thanks and all that.' I patted the pathetic girl on the shoulder. 'Honey, you've got a stronger stomach than I have,' I told her and walked out.

CHAPTER TWENTY

The evening paper played the murder up big. A go-go dancer had been slain in her apartment, without any screaming, without any burglary, but with her nude picture standing on her own dresser! What more could you want? It was seamy, it was salacious, it was delicious.

The police very carefully said there were no suspects. That's what they said. But Lasky or Metter or Jerry Nemo or Ben Schill—somebody—had let it out that Simon Kaye, a private investigator, had been seeing the girl and had picked her up from work a few hours before she was murdered.

So there was my name, big as life, weaving

an ominous path through the article, and there was Eileen, with the paper on her desk when I got in from Frank's Bar. 'The phone's been ringing all afternoon,' she said in her best reporting voice (just the facts, ma'am—only the facts). 'Every newspaper reporter in town wants an interview. So do three columnists, the local TV station, and a reporter from *The New York Times*. Also Leonard Wood called to see if you could still handle the case. I told him you could. Who else? Oh yes, two people who apparently were customers at this—ah—Frank's Bar.'

'They leave their names?'

'No. They just made threats.'

'That's it?'

'You want more?'

'There's no word from the F.B.I. or the C.I.A.?'

'Nor from the local police.' She looked at me. 'How bad is it?'

'You mean, do the cops think I did it? Not really. A couple of the less friendly ones would love it if I did, but they don't have enough evidence.'

Eileen bent over the portrait of Dana that ran on the front page of the paper and slowly and carefully said, 'Does this have to do with your search for Nerissa Claire?'

That was what she asked, but her real question was, 'Did you love her?' And when I said yes, it had to do with Nerissa Claire, some of the tension eased. She continued to study the picture, but her voice was more normal, more back to business. 'Do you know who did it, Simon?'

'No I don't.'

'Do you know *why* it was done?'

'If I knew why, I'd know who.'

'The paper doesn't give any details about her—where she came from, who she was.'

'That's the big mystery.' I dropped my notebook in front of her. 'Here's what I picked up from her application form. See how much of this can be verified, will you? It's all I could come up with at Frank's Bar. The manager doesn't know anything. I talked to the other girls there and they don't either.'

Eileen looked up at my glum face. Maybe I hadn't been in love with Dana, but I wasn't immune to her. 'It's hit you, hasn't it?' she said. 'This is why you let me give you a slug of brandy this morning.'

'Yes.'

'You want another slug?'

I decided I did.

We had one together.

Eileen said, 'I wonder what it's like to be

a go-go dancer.'

'Don't take it up. You'd be sorry.'

'How do you know?'

'I just watched a girl try out for the job, and tonight she's going to be very sorry. In fact, she might be very very sorry right about now.'

'Why? I mean, I'm very naïve.'

'Because you not only have to show off, you have to put out.'

'Oh.'

'This one, whom I just saw, is a very young kid. Tonight she's going to cry herself to sleep. Maybe tomorrow night and the next night as well. After a while, though, she'll stop crying. She'll be used to it. But she won't be the same any more.'

'How did Dana feel about it?'

'She was tough enough to fight back. They didn't break her. But that doesn't mean they didn't change her.'

'What are you going to do about it? And her?'

'Try to find out who she was. Try to find out who killed her—unless the police do it for me.'

'Any suspects?'

'There's one guy I want to talk to. I call him Lemon Eyes. He wasn't in this morning, but I'm going to lay for him. Sometime or other he's due to come home.'

'I hope you're going to leave me a name and address for him...in case he does.'

I said, 'You guessed it,' poured myself an extra slug of brandy and put the bottle away.

I didn't get back to staking out the Richard Loomis Temple to Dana Doxey until nearly eight. The intervening time was spent dodging reporters, catching up on business, saying, 'No comment,' to reporters I couldn't dodge, having some supper and a shower, answering reporters' phone calls in a Chinese accent saying, 'Mr Kaye went to Manitoba,' and having a stiff drink before I started out. Stake-outs are something you learn to endure because you have to, but they're among the worst ways in the world to pass time, especially on a street where nothing's happening. You get tired looking at the same streetlight, the same pattern of cracks in the sidewalk, the same lighted windows with only an occasional flicker to indicate that life is going on inside, the occasional car headlights flashing by. I take cigarettes with me at times like this, but not a bottle. I'd drink myself blotto in half an hour.

This was another of those nights. The windows of Loomis's shrine were black, which indicated absence, and the first hour of my watch netted no change. Had he been gone all day? Had he come in and gone out? Was he coming back tonight? Was he never coming back?

I determined I'd give him until midnight, and I watched the minutes crawl. With Dana dead, he was gone for good. I was sure of it. That dingy den of his would sit untouched until the walls fell in or the landlord got nosey. And where had Richard Loomis gone? If I wanted to find him, where would I look?

I was entertaining myself with such contemplations (which shows you how desperate one gets on a stake-out) when the light went on in his window. I'm sure as hell the smartest detective in the world. All my answers come up winners.

So Richard (Lemon Eyes) Loomis had come back after all! (Or was that someone else rustling around in there?) Funny, despite the close watch I'd been keeping—I'd thought I'd been keeping—he'd entered the building and gone to his room without my spotting him. I'd better take some more correspondence courses on how to be a detective.

I loosened and resheathed my gun so I'd be quick with it if Lemon Eye got hysterical. He was one of the unpredictables. I got out of the car and didn't slam the door. I crossed the street, entered the small building, and moved quietly into his hall. The hall was dark except for the splash of light, across the floor and up the side of the staircase that came from his open door.

I advanced in silence, braced myself on the balls of my feet, held my coat lapel with my gun hand and rapped on the door panels with the other.

There was no sound.

I pushed the door wider and there was nothing. I pushed it all the way open and stepped inside. There was a light on and that was all. The room was empty.

I turned around and there he was, standing in the doorway with a gun pointed at my chest, his yellow eyes flaming. 'You sonuvabitch,' he whispered. He came in, backing me in front of him, and I had some wild thought that he'd ultimately leave me dead under the huge blow-up picture of the dancing Dana with black tape over her nipples.

When he'd backed me as far as I could go, he stopped. He slammed the door behind him and showed me his teeth. Hate names came spewing from his mouth, and his eyes glowed amber.

'Whaddaya think,' he said, panting from the effort, bubbles of foam flecking the corners of his mouth. 'Ya think I'm dumb or something? You think I don't know your car? You think I don't know what you're doing outside my home? I'm gonna kill you. You got it coming to you for what you did to her.' He waved his gun at the pictures, showing me the 'her' he was talking about.

I had nobody to blame but myself. I was getting what I deserved. This was the guy who hid behind trees, who sneaked photographs, who spied and watched and kept out of sight. So I sit in a car he's seen across from his door, and I let him sneak into the building in front of my eyes, sucker me by turning on the light and leaving his door open, and I walk right into his arms.

'You don't want to kill me in front of her,' I said, waving at the pictures too. I had to find some tack to waylay him. I had to try, belatedly, to show a little intelligence.

'It's not yet,' he said, holding the gun with unpleasant unsteadiness. 'Not unless you make me. It's not your time yet. But it's gonna be. And when it is, nothing's gonna save you.' His grin was frighteningly unstable. I prefer a man who knows what he's about.

'You're gonna pay,' he went on. 'You're gonna pay for what you did to her.'

'I didn't kill her, if that's what you're thinking.'

'You did worse to her than killing.'

It was like that, huh? It figured.

I was sweating, but not from temperature. This sweat was cold. It was making me shiver. 'But you know who did kill her, don't you?' I said, hoping to distract him, hoping he hadn't done it himself.

He called me more names, and his aim grew shaky. I sweated some more. That wasn't the right approach.

'I wish I could do it right now,' he said in a rasping whisper. 'I've got you, right here. I could have you dead at her feet.' He looked at his gun and at me. 'But I have to wait.'

I would have liked to ask why he had to wait, but I didn't want him to think about it. He might decide the reason wasn't all that good.

So we stood, facing each other, with nothing to say. The silence made him increasingly nervous, his gun increasingly unsteady.

I took a chance. I had to do something before that gun went off. Carefully I put my hands on my head, showing that I wasn't trying any funny stuff. Slowly I started edging around the room. 'Well, if you're going to let me go for now,' I said, 'I'd better leave.'

My aim was to work my way to the door without getting close enough to him to make him react. He eyed me suspiciously, but as I moved, he moved, keeping our distance the same, keeping his gun in line with my heart, but edging away from the door, clearing the way for me.

I reached it, and our positions were reversed. Now he was back by the wall and I was in the doorway. Neither of us had said a word.

I backed into the hall and he came forward a step. He said, 'You're gonna die, mister. Remember that. And there's no way you can escape.'

I backed away from the doorway, out of his vision. I got to the outside doors, and he didn't come after me. I slipped through them and onto the stoop, then down the steps. The lights in his room were out now. He could watch me, and I couldn't see him. I was still a target.

I could have run for cover and never mind my car. I didn't. I turned my back on the building and walked slowly and casually across the street to the heap. He could shoot me down if he wanted, but I was damned if I was going to let him make me run.

CHAPTER TWENTY-ONE

So far, I was making headway like a snail in a hurricane. Saturday morning, instead of breakfast, I settled for coffee and a hangover. I don't mean I tied one on after I got home from the Lemon Eyes escapade, though I did pour myself a couple of belts. Mainly I was suffering from reaction. There were the beatings I'd taken, the murder I might have prevented, the business of being outsmarted by a simpleton like Lemon Eyes, and the frustration of not having learned a goddamn thing in three days of effort. There was also police harassment, but that isn't worth mentioning. The day I let the likes of Jake Metter and Don Lasky interfere with my digestion, I'm going to turn in my licence and peddle neckties out of a suitcase on street corners.

At half-past ten Eileen called up. That's not like Eileen. She's strictly a Gal Friday, a slave to the office five days a week, and a semi-slave to her boss. On weekends, it's another world with no carry-over. I sometimes wonder what she does, and I'm glad she doesn't know what I do, but weekends are off limits. Except that now she was on the phone saying she hoped she hadn't got me out of bed.

I wasn't sure how she meant that, but I said no, I was already up and having coffee.

'I had a feeling you wouldn't want to wait until Monday,' she said.

'For what?'

'You wanted me to check out the information on Dana Doxey's job application. You were kind of...bothered and all. I thought you'd like to know as soon as possible what I found out.'

'I would, thanks.'

'It's all make-believe. Her background is off the top of her head.'

'Schooling? Hometown? Next of kin?'

'There aren't any such places or people. The names she used as references aren't for real either.'

'Yeah, I see. Thanks.'

'I'm sorry about that. I guess it leaves you not knowing who she is.'

'It also leaves me not knowing who might have wanted to kill her and why.'

Eileen didn't dawdle. 'If there's nothing else, I have to hang up. We're going to the beach.'

She was gone, and I felt lonely. This was

not one of my good days. I wondered whom she was going to the beach with. I wished I were going to the beach.

I went to the beach with her once. Her folks invited me the summer she came to work for me. They wanted to meet the ogre who'd snapped up their little girl out of secretarial school. She wore a yellow one-piece bathing suit, very form-fitting, but also modestly cut. The other girls wore bikinis, some of them the size of postage stamps, but Eileen, in her form-fitting, modest one-piece bathing suit was the sexiest thing on the beach. I had to sit on my hands all afternoon. When I dream of Eileen, which I sometimes do, she's wearing that yellow bathing suit.

Which, of course, had nothing to do with finding Nerissa Claire or telling me who Dana Doxey was. I poured another cup of coffee and broke down and had one of those cigarettes I try not to smoke and walked around the scenario again.

There was Lemon Eyes. He was going to kill me—so he said. That wasn't a prediction that frightened me very much. A tractor trailer might kill me too, but it's not something to worry about. All you have to do is exercise a little care.

The point was, why did he choose to wait?

He could have killed me last night, but it wasn't my turn yet. Did he have to kill somebody else first? Was he doing it in order of rank? If so, who was on his list, and why?

Apart from that, what did he know about Dana's death? What might he know about Nerissa Claire? I might have found out the answers if I hadn't blown my stake-out. You're quite a detective, Kaye—a real hotshot.

Then there was Tony. He was hiding something, and it must be a pretty big something. He sure became uptight when people got curious.

There was Shelly Polk, Nerissa's supposed cousin—except she didn't behave like any cousin I'd ever known. She treated Nerissa's condo like her own while claiming she didn't know where Nerissa went. It made you wonder what never-never land Nerissa had gone to.

And, for what it was worth, Nerissa, like Dana Doxey, had a past that defied tracing.

What about Jake Metter? He was another who over-reacted when the subject of Nerissa Claire came up.

Don Lasky was still another. He was accusing me of murder an hour after Dana's body was discovered, and he didn't have more than Metter's word that I'd ever seen the girl. That was so fast I was sure he had more on me than he'd said. What was he holding back?

Lastly, there was the subject of Simon Kaye. He was supposed to go lance a few windmills, and so far all he was doing was pawing the air. Simon Kaye had better get on the ball. Leonard Wood was going to want results by ten o'clock Monday morning. But if Simon Kaye was going to produce, he had to decide what windmills to attack and get at it.

I debated the choices and decided to tackle Shelly Polk again. There were several reasons in favour of that venture. 1)Tony Manila didn't want me to; 2)Shelly Polk didn't want me to; 3)she lived in Nerissa's old pad; 4)all the things she'd told me were lies; best of all, 5)Tony might try to stop me.

I dressed in slacks, open shirt, and sneakers. I put on a hip holster and hid it under a seersucker jacket. That was as cool as I could manage, but I envied people who didn't carry guns—they didn't have to wear jackets.

This time I put the heap out of sight around a corner and reconnoitred the condo complex before making my move. That was in case Tony's Caddy was showing off its glint and glare in some handy parking slot.

There was no glint nor glare, so I moved in for a close-up inspection of Shelly's condo.

The curtains were drawn, and it looked empty.

I went up the steps and knocked. There was no answer.

Foiled again. I'd blown it with Lemon Eyes. Now it looked as if I'd blown it with Shelly. Two to one she'd been moved out and taken under Tony's wing. That was the sure way to keep me away from her.

So now, Bright Eyes, what's your next move?

That didn't take a lot of thought—not when you carry the pack of passkeys I've collected.

I let myself in, closed the door and attached the chain. It was dim inside with the curtains drawn. It was also uninhabited and gave the feeling it would be empty for a long while.

There was no hurry, and I went through it at my leisure. It was an elegant pad and, as I said before, not the sort of digs a cop can pay the rent on and still put food on the table. It wasn't the place a go-go dancer can afford either, unless she's been getting bigger tips than the Frank's Bar clientele can pass out.

It was a Tony Manila-type hangout. He could stake Nerissa to this kind of life. And he used to go with her. But that had ended, and she had gone with Matt Brent.

The pieces didn't fit. If Nerissa Claire had a Tony Manila in tow, what would she want with a Matt Brent? And why would she continue to go-go dance? She'd only plug away at her dancing and go with the Matt Brents of the world if the Tony Manilas gave her the heave-ho. But Tony looked very much still in the picture.

I frowned and stroked my chin and prowled through the drawers and closets.

There were no suitcases. Shelly had decamped with those. But a lot of the rest of the stuff was right there on display—clothes in the closet...enough to dress the needy of India—with chiffon, rayon and nylon goodies in all the drawers. Shelly might have loaded some suitcases, but it would take a moving van to cart the whole wardrobe.

All this was very interesting, but the question was: whose clothes were they? It would take a girl with a sugar daddy the better part of a year to accumulate such an array of finery, and Shelly hadn't been here long enough. On the other hand, Matt Brent couldn't have provided so much. Without an outside income he couldn't meet the rent payments on the apartment. So where did the money come from, and to whom did it go?

Then there was something else—a framed picture on the dresser, an outdoorsy picture with snow on the ground and a couple of people done up to the eyeballs in woollens and furs, holding a pair of skis apiece. One was Shelly Polk, her face framed in mink, a cat's grin on her face. The man with her, who looked as if he'd swallowed a couple of canaries himself, was Tony Manila.

Well, what do you know? Maybe Shelly'd been collecting a wardrobe longer than I'd thought. The mystery deepened.

On the strength of that, I made a visit to all the neighbouring condominiums. As I say, they're structured for maximum privacy, and no window overlooks a neighbour's door, meaning you have to have a real nose for news to keep tabs on who comes and goes in those places. However, you never can tell, you might be lucky.

I was lucky in one respect. I caught all the neighbours snug in their homes or working on their little patches of grass and garden. I wasn't lucky with what I got. Nobody could give me more than a smattering of information.

Nerissa Claire? Is that the name of the woman in 4A? Young brunette girl? Pretty figure? Never saw her close up. A large man called on her from time to time. At least he looked like he went to her place. And she came out with him from time to time. Oh, she hasn't lived here very long—six months, maybe a year. No, I haven't seen her recently.

There's another woman in there now, a blond woman. I haven't met her. I guess Miss Claire moved out. The blond woman? Yeah, she seems to date—seen a dark-haired young man with her a couple of times—flashy dresser, big car, seems to have money.

That was that, and what was what? I still didn't know what the pieces meant or how to put the puzzle together.

CHAPTER TWENTY-TWO

I brought the picture of the fur-clad couple back with me to my condo. I thought it would be an interesting item to show around. There were a few expressions on a few faces I'd like to watch.

As a matter of record, the first person to see it wasn't anyone I intended to show it to. He wasn't on my list at all. In fact, I didn't really show it to him. He took it away from me.

I came up the grade to pull into my slot beside my storm porch, and I caught a peek of a white Porsche tucked away around one of the other buildings. There's only one guy in town with that particular plate number—Jake Metter.

That's enough to spoil your lunch. He wasn't in sight, though, and I hoped it wasn't me he was after, that maybe he was only out arresting little tots for drag racing their kiddie cars.

No such luck. When I left the heap and went around to the steps, out he jumped from behind the corner. That's called 'the element of surprise,' which is supposed to give the cop the advantage. He must have read it in the handbook.

'Well,' he said, confronting me, hands on hips, chest thrust out to increase his bulk (that's called 'intimidation' and it's also in the handbook). 'Just getting in, huh? Big night, huh?'

Then, before I could answer, he snatched the picture out of my hand. 'What've you got here? Where'd you get this?' He took a look and stared. There they were, Tony and Shelly with skis, ready for an afternoon on the slopes, but I couldn't tell from his expression whether he knew who they were, didn't know people did that sort of thing, or deduced that they weren't relatives of mine. In any case, after the stare, he frowned like God and said, 'Where'd you get this?'

I said, 'Woolco's. Two for a dollar.'

He almost smashed it in my face. 'What are you doing with this picture? Who'd you steal it from?'

I pretended I didn't hear that. I held out my hand and said, 'If you give it back to me quietly and go away, I'll pretend you didn't take it from me.'

He worked to control himself. 'I asked you a question. When I ask you a question, you answer it.'

I nearly laughed, but managed to give him no more than an incredulous stare. 'You've got to be kidding. You've really got to be kidding.'

'Where've you been all night?' He glanced at my trousers. 'Got any bloodstains on your clothes?'

'Only where I cut myself shaving. Give me my picture and get the hell off my steps.'

Metter took a deep breath, and of course he didn't get off my steps. 'You're in up to your neck,' he said. 'You don't want to tell me where you were last night? That's okay, you don't have to. But the boys downtown are going to ask you questions you're damned well going to answer. And if you don't believe me, call your goddamn lawyer.' He jerked a thumb at my car. 'Get back behind the wheel, smart boy. We're going downtown together, and then we'll see how many smart-ass remarks you can come up with.'

'Are you placing me under arrest?'

'You can damn well consider yourself lucky if we don't.'

'Well, when you do, you can take me downtown. In the meantime, give me back my picture and get off my property.'

'This ain't your picture. I know damned well this ain't your picture. You stole it, didn't you? This is stolen property and you know it.'

I held out my hand for it. 'You're wasting my time and the taxpayers' money. Either arrest me and I'll go downtown with you, or leave me alone.'

'You're stalling,' he said. 'You think by refusing to go downtown unless you're under arrest you can get out of answering questions. You've got a lot of answering to do, Mr Hotshot, and you aren't going to get out of it by pulling out the rule book and relying on a lot of technicalities.'

'I'll answer questions, but not downtown. Bring your damned stenographers and high-powered interrogators out here.' I leaned on the railing. 'By the way, who am I supposed to have killed this time?'

Metter thrust the picture into my hands. 'Don't worry,' he said. 'They'll come out. And you'd better be here when they do.'

He stalked off toward the hidden Porsche to radio in.

They did come out—Metter, a couple of other patrolmen, a stenographer (which made it serious) and, in charge of the operation, Detective Sergeant Don Lasky again, his face still puffy and bruised from where I'd whacked him night before last. With all the people in the department, I kept getting Metter and Lasky. I'd've thought Lasky would want no more of me than I wanted of him!

We held the party in my living room, and I served coffee. This time, though Metter scowled up a storm, Lasky was subdued. Maybe it was the bruises he carried, maybe he'd learned I didn't crumble under pressure. Either way, he wasn't going to accuse me of the crime until we'd talked about it a little.

First he wanted to know what I'd been doing last night. (That's S.O.P for the police. Ask questions, but don't say why you want the answers.)

'What time last night?'

Lasky was subdued but that doesn't mean he was toothless. He pursed his lips. 'Let's say,' he answered evilly, 'after your altercation with a young man named Richard Loomis.'

'Altercation?'

'It was a hot night last night. Everybody had windows open. Voices carry. You and Mr Loomis were heard in argument. In fact, he was overheard threatening to kill you. Do you want to tell us about it?'

'Not unless it's relevant to what I'm supposed to have been doing the rest of the night. That's the part you want to know about, isn't it?'

'We think it's relevant,' Lasky said. 'We think it's relevant any time one person threatens the life of another person.'

'But he threatened me. I didn't threaten him.'

'And why did he threaten you?'

'Ask him.'

'We'd rather ask you.'

'Is that so? Let me guess. You want me to tell you, because you can't get the answer from Mr Loomis. That's because Mr Loomis is dead and can't talk. Isn't that right? And you don't really think I killed him, but you don't have anybody else, and you're hoping against hope you might get lucky and make a connection. How'm I batting?'

'It's interesting,' Lasky said, 'how you come up with answers before we even ask the questions. It makes us wonder how come you know so much.'

'I spent enough time doing what you're doing to learn the routine.'

'And you still haven't told us what you did last night after Richard Loomis chased you out of his place.'

'I came home here in a cold sweat and went to bed with a stiff drink.'

Lasky laughed. He elbowed Metter to get him to share his mirth. 'That's right,' he said. 'Simon Kaye comes home with his tail between his legs, scared to death by this pipsqueak of a punk, Richard Loomis.' He pointed a finger. 'You know what kind of a guy you are, Kaye? Not like that. You're the kind of guy who would resent a punk pulling a gun and threatening you. You'd lay for him. That's what you'd do. You'd want to pay him back, because you want to present a macho image. And you'd have a second reason. If you kill him, then he can't kill you.'

'Where'd I kill him, by the way?'

'You tell us. All we know is where you dumped him.'

'I dumped him, eh? What'd I use for transport? My car? You want to test it for bloodstains?'

Lasky arched an eyebrow. 'You know there was blood then?'

'Metter gave it away. Blame it on him.'

'What was the quarrel about? Dana Doxey, wasn't it?'

I said, 'Now I get it. The Dana Doxey case is yours, and he had all those pictures of her, so you're into this one too. How was he murdered?'

'Interesting pictures, weren't they? They had a kind of religious connotation to them, didn't they?'

'Maybe he liked her soul.'

'But not someone like you,' Lasky went on. 'A girl's soul wouldn't interest you. The body's the thing, right, Kaye?'

The muscles in my face got tight. Was he going to try that again?

'What do *you* think, Jake?' he went on to Metter when I didn't answer. 'You think Kaye's the soul type or the body type?'

'He'd screw anything in a skirt.'

'What about that Dana Doxey? You think he'd go for something like that?'

'She was a slut. Of course he would.'

I got to my feet. 'Up out of that chair,' I said to Metter. 'I blacked Lasky's eye for that. I'm going to black yours.'

It was Lasky who rose. He got between us. 'Next time you try it, you're in jail. Remember who we are.'

'Any more cracks,' I said, 'and I'll throw

him through the window, and I don't care *who* you are.'

'You going to her funeral?' Metter said, stretching his legs. 'You'll be the only one.'

I said to Lasky, 'Get him on his feet.'

Lasky blocked me with his body. 'He didn't say anything. He only asked if you were going to her funeral.'

'I heard him.'

Metter said, 'It's going to be a pauper's grave. No service. Bring your Bible and read her a psalm.'

I pushed Lasky out of the way. He grabbed me. 'For Christ's sake, will you keep your head?' To Metter, he said, 'Lay off.'

I broke Lasky's grasp. 'That tears it,' I said. 'Out. The lot of you.'

'All right,' Lasky grumbled. 'He shouldn't've ridden you like that. We're only trying to get information. We've got two killings. The Doxey girl and Richard Loomis. We want to know who did it. You're connected to the two of them. You can't blame us for coming around.'

'I blame you for your tactics. I blame you for bringing that creep with you.' I gestured at Metter. 'Hereafter, keep him away from me or I'll shove his badge down his throat.'

'Oh, hell,' Lasky said, 'that's only tactics.

218

He was needling you to get you to say things. Hell, you know the tricks as well as I do.'

'And he can practise them on someone else. And while we're at it, what's this business about Dana and a pauper's grave? Is that one of his tricks?'

Lasky shook his head. 'Of course not. That's on the level.'

'Why? What's it all about?'

Lasky said, 'Well, hell, don't blame me. There's no score on her. Her poop sheet was make-believe. Nobody knows who she is or where she came from. There's nobody to bury her except the city. So what do you want the taxpayers to buy her as a going-away present, a mausoleum? It's potter's field for the unclaimed bodies. What did you expect?'

CHAPTER TWENTY-THREE

I looked up Jack McGuire in the late afternoon—Father Jack, if you prefer. He's the parish priest, the guy I grew up with, fought with, talk with, play chess with on Monday nights—that sort of thing. He's a priest and

I'm a heathen, but we do agree on some things. Anyway, he's a helluva good guy to have in your corner no matter where he goes to church—or where you go.

I tried the manse or rectory or whatever you call it. That's not where Jack's going to be on a Saturday afternoon, but it's where Mrs Honeywell, his houskeeper, could clue me in. He was out coaching the church school girls' softball team.

I found him out in the field back of the graveyard behind the church. There were these thirteen- and fourteen-year-old girls out there, swinging bats, fielding balls and learning to throw with a full-arm sweep. They were cute as hell, which is probably the wrong thing to say in *now* circles, but that's how they looked to me.

Jack, in a baseball cap, wearing a T-shirt with the legend Only Steal Bases on the back, was hitting out fungoes, telling the girls, 'Girl on first,' or 'First and second, one out,' or 'Girl on third, two out,' and the kids responded accordingly—or they were supposed to.

I watched for five minutes before he saw me. Then he said 'What're you doing here? You already know this game.'

I said, 'Look at those kids gobble up your grounders. No wonder you never made the majors.'

'But don't they look great?' he said proudly. 'We're going to clean up in the church league this summer. We're four and oh already.' He lashed a sharp liner at the shortstop. It hit at shoe-top level and she fell over backward, but she held it. She arched it to first base on her knees and Jack said, 'She's my star. She's going to be really good.'

He handed the bat to the tall girl catching the throw-ins, told her to keep it going, and walked me to the sidelines where he poured lemonade from a thermos. I declined a cupful, which he gulped and set down. 'So what do you want?'

I said, 'How're you fixed for burial plots?'

'Tight. Why? Who's to be buried?'

I told him about Dana, what she'd done for me, what had happened to her, but not who she was. 'Nobody knows who she was,' I explained. 'Her job application, her career reports—they're all phony. As a result, nobody knows where she belongs, or whom she belongs to?'

'And you're looking for a place for her remains?'

'Roughly speaking, yes.'

'Was she Catholic?'

'If I could tell you that much, I could tell you the rest and I wouldn't be wasting our

221

time. I don't play softball anymore—even girls' softball—only chess.'

'You want something to go with a burial plot then? A service?'

'If you could provide such things.'

He said seriously, 'I don't know, Simon. I'll have to check it out. But if I'm going to do a service for a girl, I'd like to know something about her. I don't like stock ceremonies where you fill in the blank with the name of the deceased. It's meaningless.'

'She was a go-go dancer at Frank's Bar and she told me once she aspired to be a porno queen, but I wouldn't want you to talk about her that way.'

Jack shook his head. 'Trust you to bring up her best points. What about the people she worked with? They'd know something about her.'

'I talked to them. They know from nothing.'

'I don't mean her background, I mean the kind of a girl she was.'

'I can tell you that. Never mind the porno-queen stuff, she was a nice kid.'

'Sure she was, but that tells me nothing. I'd like to hear a woman's view of her. How about if I talk to the other girls who dance there.'

'I'd like to have you.'

He called to the lanky kid on second. 'That's

not the way to throw. Sweep your arm. It's got to be a continuous motion—the same when you bat.' To me, he said, always with an eye on his young charges, 'When's a good time to see the other dancers?'

'See them or talk to them?'

'Come on, you clown. You're in it, too. You've got to introduce me.'

I said, 'They work in shifts, but I have to tell you the manager won't like them talking to priests between appearances. They're supposed to hustle drinks from the customers.'

'And we wouldn't want to interfere with the manager's peace of mind, would we?'

'Or the girls' livelihood. They get a cut of the take.'

'What do you suggest?'

'The first girl goes off at eleven, the other two at one a.m.'

'Why don't I meet you there at ten-thirty? That way I can get the feel of the place, and you can pave the way for me to talk with them at their convenience.'

I said that would do fine.

'I still can't promise you a plot,' he said, 'but I can give you a service.'

CHAPTER TWENTY-FOUR

I got to Frank's Bar at ten and moved in near the back. This was Saturday night, and even with the air conditioning the room was hot and thick with smoke and people. The girl on the stand doing the bare-breasted number was Jean Smith, the brunette beauty whose audition I'd watched yesterday afternoon, the one whose stomach was stronger than mine. She was swaying and shaking, and all she wore was a bikini bottom cut so low it could only have been held up by hope. Now I could see why Ben Schill wanted her to pull down her pants. His bar hadn't gone bottomless yet, but if it did, she'd lead the way.

Her body was slinky and provocative, even if she didn't yet know how to be sensual, and she was really packing them in. She'd worked up a sweat trying to prove herself, and her skin glistened under the spot, and I thought of Dana when I noted that none of the perspiration was dripping off her nipples. From the neck down she was sexy without knowing how. From the neck up, she was dead. She wore a pasted smile, but her face had as much expression as a mannequin's. Her eyes were blank and stared over the heads of the voyeurs as if she were looking for tomorrow. I wondered if she'd been worked over by Ben Schill and his friends after her audition. Something had happened to her in the last twenty-four hours. She looked as if she'd just discovered that sewers lie under the streets of Paris and was making an adjustment. It was a different face from yesterday's, and I felt sad for her. But let's not get maudlin. It's the way of the world...one of the ways.

I checked out the dim eager male faces surrounding me. Joe Dirk and Jimmy Neeley, a couple of off-duty cops, were against the wall and I edged over. Their eyes were popping, and I said, 'Going to wait for the next show before you raid the place?'

Joe gave me a glassy-eyed gaze and said to Jimmy, 'Jeez, she even draws private detectives. How classy can you get?'

Jimmy said to him, 'You ought to read the papers, Joe. The papers say he goes out with the girls and everything.'

Joe turned serious. 'Lasky give you a hard time on the Doxey killing?'

I said, 'That'll be the day.'

'He should know better than try to tie you

in on a homicide like that.'

'Know better? When did he ever?'

Jimmy watching the dancer, said, 'Between you and all the publicity this place's getting, we thought we should check it out.'

I said, 'You mean you're in here on your own time? Frank's Bar is still operating within the limits.'

'No complaints so far.' Jimmy answered. 'But if that bikini rides down about one-half an inch, I expect the Legion of Decency will be on our backs.'

Joe said, 'Legion of Decency? I thought that went out with pasties. Remember when girls had to wear pasties?'

I said, 'No, but I'm younger than you are.'

Jimmy said, 'Hey, a priest just came in. Do you suppose he's here to evaluate the height of that bikini?'

'That's Jack McGuire,' Joe told him. 'In his parish, that's got to be the least of his worries.'

I said, 'He's looking for lost sheep like me,' and I worked my way in his direction.

He saw me coming, turned and watched as the girl named Sassie mounted the bar top to replace Jean. Sassie removed the cape from her pendulous breasts while Jean slipped into a robe and picked her way down the small steps to applause and cheers. Jean Smith had a future. What it would be, I wouldn't try to guess, but no question she had a future.

Sassie wasn't pleased. She put her hands on her head and swung her shoulders, bouncing her breasts out as far as she could.

Jack McGuire watched the other girl descend. He said, 'Raw meat on the hoof for the delight of the customers. Her popularity doesn't seem to bring her much happiness.'

I said, 'The trouble with you is you feel sorry for everybody.'

'Is she one of the ones I'm to talk to?'

'She didn't know the dead girl. She's her replacement.'

'Who else is there?'

'That's Sassie, up on the stage. She's Nerissa's replacement. The other girl, Lucille, is over there, at that table, sitting with the fat man. She's got her hand on his knee.'

'You cops!' he said.

'Ex-cop. What's your problem?'

'You not only spot the girl, you know what she's doing with her hands. Who else would notice a thing like that?'

'You don't watch where the magician points. You watch where he doesn't point.'

Jack looked back up at the platform where Sassie gyrated, her breasts flopping around. He said, 'What a helluva way to make a living.'

'There are worse.'

'This is what the dead girl did?'

'Same job. She was better at it.'

'And she was special to you.'

'She was. Which is why I want her in a proper plot, not a pauper's grave.'

He watched Sassie some more. She was closing her eyes and licking her lips, pretending she was in the heat of passion, but she was more funny than sexy. He said, 'When does she get through?'

'After this stretch. She's off at eleven. I'll see if we can all go someplace together and talk.'

'Perhaps a few minutes with her in her dressing room would be all I'd need.'

'As you like it.'

I brought him with me through the thick crowd to the dressing-room door and gave it Ben Schill's code knock. Jean Smith, her robe clutched at her throat, fear in her eyes, looked out. It wasn't Ben Schill standing there, and fear turned to relief. She said, 'Don't I know you?'

'I was at your audition yesterday.'

Recognition glimmered. 'Oh, yes. You walked out. You didn't want to see the good part.'

'I didn't want to see what would happen *after* the good part.'

Her smile was like a boxer's when he's been

punched too hard. 'It was a ball,' she said. 'We all had a ball. Especially me! I got the job.'

'You look very happy.'

'Sure I'm happy.' A sick look crossed her face subliminally fast, and the smile was back, bright and hard as a diamond. She pulled the door open. 'Well, come on in, if you don't mind my dressing. What can I do for you?'

We wanted to see Sassie, I explained, and we could wait outside. She wouldn't hear of it and pulled us inside desperately. 'Ben's drilled it into us we have to be sociable. We're not just to be gazed at from afar, he says. I wouldn't want him to think I'm not friendly.'

She sat us on the couch, took off her robe and got into her dress, asking us with the uncertainty of an aspiring actress how we liked her performance. The dress she got into and straightened in front of the mirror was the one she'd taken off in Ben's office the preceding afternoon, except that it was one day dirtier. 'I've got to go now,' she explained after primping her hair. 'I've got to mingle with the customers. If Ben comes around looking for me, tell him I'm mingling. Make sure you tell him that. He doesn't think I know how to mingle.'

We said we'd tell him and she went out. Jack looked after her sadly, sniffed the stale perfume and viewed the shabby decor. 'Sometimes I think it's a losing battle,' he said. 'I teach my girls to play softball and I see how eager they are, and how happy, and I feel pretty good. Then I come to a place like this and I get depressed. There're so many more bars than churches.'

'Cheer up. Not many of them are as sleazy as this.'

'But it packs them in...or the girls do.' He turned my way. 'This is a favourite hangout of yours?'

'Of mine?'

'You know the girls, you know the secret knock.'

'I'm working on a case, you cluck.'

We had ten minutes to absorb the atmosphere before the next interruption. That was Lucille coming back from her customer. She turned a key, walked in, greeting me without surprise and doing only the slightest double take at finding a priest in her boudoir.

I introduced him and explained that he was interested in what Dana Doxey was like, and maybe she could answer a few questions.

She pulled her dress over her head, which left her with nothing on but her costume. 'Fire away,' she said, putting her dress on a hanger and sitting down in front of the vanity mirror to powder her breasts and make up her face. 'But I've only got a minute.'

Jack, watching the process dispassionately, suggested it might be better if we discussed Dana when she had more time.

'Suits me,' she said, getting up and donning her cape. She disappeared out the passageway without a goodbye.

We were alone for another minute, then Sassie came in, shedding her robe until she saw she had company. She pulled it back around her and said, 'Oh, for Christ's sake, it's a goddam convention.' To me, she said, 'What're you bringing a goddam priest around for? You think he's going to preach me out of a job?'

I made introductions and explained that Father McGuire wasn't here to close the joint or save her soul, he only wanted to talk to her about Dana Doxey.

'What the hell for? I told you yesterday I don't know anything about the broad except that she's dead.'

'He's not after background, he just wants to talk to people who knew her. He's going to conduct a service for her. We don't want to have her just dumped into a pauper's grave.'

Sassie turned maudlin. 'Poor Dana,' she said and wiped her mascara.

I said I'd leave them alone, shut the door behind me, and went around to watch listless Lucille do her thing.

In three minutes Jack rejoined me, shaking his head. 'She's no help. She hates all the other girls. Doesn't have anything to do with them. Are they all that unfriendly and un-communicative?'

'I don't know, but it's possible. Dana lived for a couple of months with an ex-go-go dancer I'm trying to trace and learned absolutely nothing about her.' I nodded at the platform and the gyrating dancer. 'Do you still want to talk to Lucille, or is it a waste of time?'

'We've come this far, we might as well go the rest of the way.'

'She doesn't get through until one. Do you want to wait or buy her a drink?'

'I'd rather wait. But not here. Let's go find a bite to eat.'

We went outside, away from the smoke and heat and smell, from the bare female bodies and the lusting male eyes. It was cooler outside. A quick summer shower had wet down the pave-ments, and the world had a fresh, clean scent.

There was a fast-food emporium across the street, and we had just started for it when Jack let out a yelp and jumped at me. He's big, and when he hits, you know it. He knocked me off my feet, and I crashed to the pavement with him on top.

I was going to say, 'What the hell,' but I didn't have a chance. Before we landed, three loud explosions rang out and I heard the whistle of bullets.

I came down on my right shoulder, rolled between parked cars, and had my gun in my hand by the time I came to rest.

For a moment there was nothing but stillness. Then, up the road, the gunman broke from cover and went for the corner like a forty-yard-dash man coming off the starting blocks.

My first shot missed. I hurried it. I ought to know better, but that's what I did. I held the gun steady the second time and took careful aim, even though he was almost too far away and moving fast. I squeezed off a round, and patience paid off. He didn't drop, but he staggered. Then he was around the corner, and I was up on one knee.

Jack was lying on the sidewalk. He hadn't rolled to safety like I had. I crawled to him and shook his shoulder.

He said, 'I've been hit.'

CHAPTER TWENTY-FIVE

'Don't move. Lie still,' I said.

I folded my jacket under his head for a pillow. I was pretty scared. Around us people poured out of Frank's Bar as if it were on fire, all jabbering and gathering around, wanting to know what happened.

I yelled at them to stand back and call an ambulance. I felt for Jack's pulse and kept talking to him, asking about pain, if he knew where he'd been hit. The crowd kept saying, 'Jeez, it's the priest. The priest's been shot.' Jack said he didn't feel anything, just weak.

I found his pulse. It was strong, but you never know about those things. The main artery goes down the inside of the backbone, and if you get a hole in that artery, you're dead.

Joe Dirk and Jimmy Neeley pushed through. When a fella needs a friend, it's nice if he's also a cop. Cops know what to do. Joe went for the ambulance, and Jimmy helped me open up Jack's clothes.

'Pulse strong,' Neeley announced. 'You'll

be okay, Father.' To me, he said, 'Who did it?'

'A man. Six-footer. Dark suit. Something black over his face.'

'Black man, maybe?'

'No. His hands were white.'

'Got any enemies, Father? Know who'd like to kill you?'

Jack shook his head and said nothing. He knew, as I knew, that the slug had been aimed my way and he'd taken it to shield me. But he wasn't telling that to the police. If I wanted them to know, I could tell them.

Jimmy and I located the wound. It was upper chest, under the clavicle, and it might have fractured the scapula and nicked a rib, but it hadn't hit anything vital. I made a compress out of my handkerchief and held it there. I was feeling better about things.

Jimmy was relieved too. He got back to business. 'Where'd the guy shoot from?'

I pointed. 'He came out of the shadows there, cut loose with three rounds, then ran around the corner—limped around the corner.'

'Limped?'

'I winged him. Right leg.'

'You think he's down? You think he's still there?'

'I don't think he was hurt that bad. But if the T.P.F does a search, they might find a blood trail or someone who saw where he went.'

Jimmy nodded. 'I'll recommend it. And we'll check the hospitals for bullet wounds.' He went off for a phone.

In the distance there was an ambulance siren. I checked my compress for bleeding and re-applied it. Jack grinned at me and said thanks for the pillow, he hoped he wasn't getting blood on it.

I told him he was a big palooka who ought to learn to move away from bullets instead of into them. He said, 'I'm glad you didn't get hit,' and I said that if I had, I wouldn't be here to talk about it. 'He was firing from a distance, but he had me nailed. I was dead centre in his sights when you threw that block.'

The sirens were loud now. Bright lights were flashing, and the crowd gave way.

I rode in the ambulance with Jack. The attendants said no, and I was going to punch them out, but Jack said yes, and that settled it. He didn't even have to raise his voice. A clerical collar sure smooths a lot of the rough-ness out of life. (Or maybe it was the bullet wound.)

For the record, the doctors operated on him within the hour, and had the bullet out and

Jack in the recovery room by half-past three Sunday morning.

As for me, I didn't get to him until much later. First, I had to call his housekeeper and a few other essential people he had numbers for. Second, the police swarmed over the hospital like a plague of blue ants. A very popular priest had been gunned down. A private detective named Simon Kaye had reputedly wounded the assailant and had been a witness. Simon Kaye was expected to provide answers to a lot of questions.

The Tactical Police Force did the search I'd suggested. They questioned residents in the area, pounding on doors, waking the neighbourhood, asking about the gunshots—and all the rest of the T.P.F tactic.

A couple of people had actually seen the guy limping and hopping down the street, but they couldn't describe him or tell where he went. The T.P.F even backed that up with several small bloodstains on the sidewalk. Unfortunately the stains didn't form a trail. That left the police without a suspect and without a motive. I was supposed to provide them with both.

'What were you doing in the company of a Catholic priest outside of a go-go bar in the downtown area of the city?' Detective Ed Chardy was asking the questions.

'He and I grew up together.'

'Were you in Frank's Bar together?'

'Yes.'

'What were you doing there?'

'Watching the go-go dancers.'

'What did Father McGuire go to Frank's Bar to watch go-go dancers for?'

'Ask him.'

'Why did you go?'

'I like to watch go-go dancers.'

'Come on, for Christ's sake, will you level with us? Joe Dirk and Jimmy Neeley saw you there. They saw you meet Father McGuire. They say you went to the girls' dressing room, the two of you.'

'Then what're you talking to me for? Why don't you talk to them?'

'Come on, Simon, dammit. Stop playing ring-around-the-rosy. Nobody's accusing you of anything. We know you're in on what's going on. We know you knew the girl who was murdered the other night. We've got witnesses who saw you with her, and she was carrying your business card in her purse. But you're not under suspicion. Stop thinking you're under suspicion.'

My mouth popped open. 'What did you say? My business card was in her purse?'

'Yeah, but we don't count that as anything...'

That had to be the extra evidence Lasky had on me. But how had she got it? 'Wait a second,' I said. 'I never gave her my card. She didn't get it from *me*!'

'All right, don't get excited. I never said she did. I'm just saying you know these people and you can help us out—'

'If she didn't get it from me, it came from someone else. Maybe her killer planted it in her purse. Maybe—'

'Maybe you should tell it to Don Lasky. He's in charge of the Doxey case. Dammit, I'm trying to solve a shooting—an attempt on Father McGuire's life.'

'Lasky? He couldn't find A in the alphabet.'

'Or was it an attempt on your life? Will you, for Chrissake, level with us?'

I'd think about the card later. It wasn't Chardy's department. He was on the Father McGuire shooting. I sighed and said, 'If I levelled with you, you wouldn't believe me.'

'Try me.'

'All right,' I said. 'A go-go dancer named Dana Doxey was killed the day before yesterday about this time. She's the one who you say was carrying my business card.'

'I know, I know.'

'I hear she's going to be buried in a pauper's

grave. I knew her, and I don't want that. I asked Father McGuire to give her a proper burial.
He went to Frank's Bar with me to examine
the situation before making a decision—before
going to whomever makes those decisions.'

Chardy was an old-timer from my own days
on the force. He had a leathery mobile face and
the slightest expression set all his muscles in
motion. Now his smile split his face in two. He
stroked a raffish chin. 'So you and the Father
went to Frank's Bar for, shall we say, socio-
logical purposes?'

'You can say that if you want.'

'And you walk outside, for a breath of fresh
air, perhaps, and somebody tries to kill you?
Is that it?'

'That certainly seemed to me to be it.'

'Which one of you do you figure he was trying to kill?'

'I'm no mind reader.'

'The two of you are "innocently" watching
go-go dancers? So after you've had your fill,
as it were, you step outside. And the moment
you do, a guy comes out of the shadows and
goes "boom boom." And Father McGuire is
seriously wounded and you, quick on the trigger as usual, put a hit on the gunman who
leaves a few drops of blood behind as a
souvenir. Is that your story?'

'No, that's *your* story.'

'And you want to know something? I don't believe it.'

I said, 'I told you you wouldn't.'

He held out beckoning fingers. 'Come on, Simon. Let's have it for real. For once in your life—'

That's when I told him to go to hell.

They put Jack in bed in a four-patient room at half-past five and gave him something to make him sleep. That's where he was when I got back to him, when I'd finally shaken Chardy and the rest of the cops. He was asleep by then, and I slept too, in a chair by his bed.

When I next awoke, it was noon and Jack was taking nourishment. He told me to go to bed, and the glint in his eye said he was almost okay. I said I'd get some sleep and bring in my chess set.

He said, 'While you're at it, bring in the name of the man who shot me.'

'You want to belt him?'

'I want to forgive him.'

'I don't know why I even talk to you.'

CHAPTER TWENTY-SIX

I got swarmed over with reporters and parish-
ioners on my way to the elevator. The parish-
ioners wanted to know the condition of Father
McGuire, the reporters wanted the details of
the shoot-out. I told batch one that Father
was fine and batch two that some sonuvabitch
had opened fire on us and I winged him in
return, but not where it would do me the
most good.

'Get a good look at him?'

'No.'

'Know who he was?'

'No.'

'Any idea?'

'No. If you want to know his identity, you
should be down at police headquarters. Hospitals and doctors who treat gunshot wounds
report it to the police, not to me.'

'We did that,' one reporter growled. 'There's
no reports.'

'Maybe you only *thought* you hit him,' another said. 'You wantta change your story?'

I said, 'So's your old man,' and boarded the car.

So the doctor who treated the wounded gunman hadn't reported it to the authorities? Maybe some money had changed hands instead. The world doesn't turn according to Hoyle.

That info saved me calling the cops myself, and I was left with time on my hands. What to do?

What I felt like doing was going home and sacking out for a few hours. What I did do was buy a thirty-four billionth hamburger from McDonald's, roll the heap over to Vincent Manila's luxury estate, park where I wouldn't be seen, and settle down to the tedium of another stake-out. Seeing as how Tony Manila hated my guts and had enough money to bribe doctors, I thought I'd see if he was walking with a limp. I mean, that's being a smart detective.

If you want to think of fun things to do, sit in a car with a steel roof under a hot sun on the longest day of the year and watch the empty driveway of a huge estate that's behind a wall and swallowed by trees. The glare of the sun shimmered off the pavements, the people stayed indoors, and hardly a car had the energy to pass by. I'd removed my jacket when I left the frigidly conditioned air of the hospital, and now I removed my tie, rolled up my sleeves and unbuttoned my shirt. It didn't do any good. My shirt turned to water, rivulets ran down my chest and back. Usually I wear my gun on my hip, though I've got both kinds of holsters. I removed my holster and put it on my jacket. I undid my belt. I thought about the way my business card might have found its way into Dana's purse, but that only made my brain hurt. I thought about buying a six-pack of beer, but it was Sunday. I thought about ice-cream sodas and water fountains. I thought of swimming pools and open fire hydrants. Then I thought about mushing through a blizzard to the North Pole.

At half-past three there was some action. A black chauffeur-driven limousine pulled out of the drive and headed the other way. I couldn't get a good look at the passengers, but I counted four.

The limo went smoothly over the pavement, not breaking any speed records, just cruising modestly, enjoying the scenery behind closed windows: the air-conditioned filthy rich out for a Sunday drive.

The drive ended at the Alderberry Cemetery, the one with all the mausoleums, statues, and three-ton headstones. No pikers admitted. The limo swung in past the gatehouse and I followed it over the rise down to the big marble sepulchres at the end. It was just a visit to the family tomb to lay flowers on the coffins.

I took a branch road and parked where I had a good view. By the time I did, the chauffeur had helped Tony out of the back. And he needed help. He was on a crutch and keeping his right leg off the ground. He was my boy, all right. That was the leg I'd hit.

After Tony came his mother, a baby dirigible dressed in a black tent decorated with giant velvet bows.

The father followed—that would be Vincent Manila. He took Tony's left arm, marching him along while the wife tottered after on spike heels and piano legs.

Coming last and least was Shelly Polk, and the chauffeur's assist was perfunctory. Judging from the handling, she rated below the salt.

Tony got dragged about four steps before turning balky. He shook off the old man's hand and waited for Shelly. Ma and Pa kept going.

In strung-out fashion they reached the door of a marble and bronze mausoleum: Pa first, Ma at his heels, Tony and Shelly making slow progress together, and lastly the chauffeur with a large basket of flowers he'd retrieved from the front seat. Pa had keys and, after a bit, he got the door open and the party moved inside.

What did all that tell me? It removed all doubt as to who'd plugged Jack McGuire. And he'd been aiming at me. Which meant he'd be back after me again as soon as he could make his right foot touch ground. The other thing I learned was that Shelly wasn't the family favourite—if that was something worth knowing. Back to the drawing board.

I stopped by police headquarters on my return to try my luck. My luck was good. Dan Saxton was on the desk. I said, 'I've got a hot tip on the Father McGuire shooting.'

'You mean it?'

'I mean it's a tip. It's not evidence, it's not proof.'

'What's the tip?'

'A guy by the name of Tony Manila has his right leg bandaged. The guy who plugged McGuire caught a slug in the right leg.'

'What says it isn't coincidence?'

'I've had run-ins with Tony before. He was my choice for the job even before I found he had a bad leg.'

'What kind of run-ins?'

'A couple of tiffs over my prying into his affairs.'

'You swearing out a complaint?'

'Don't be a jerk.'

'The Manilas are an important family. We wouldn't want to make any mistake.'

'Their money's in auto maintenance, repairs, body work, engines, you name it. Were they investigated in that stolen car ring, or are they too high up?'

Dan said, 'Oh, hell, Simon, nobody's that high up. That ring was big. Everybody was under suspicion.'

'They were investigated?'

'Hell, yes. We even pulled a surprise raid, which they're threatening to sue us over. They were clean. Everybody was clean. That was the trouble. We don't know who was doing it or how. But it was done.'

'You keep using the past tense. Why?'

'The thefts have almost completely stopped. Car thefts have dropped eighty-five percent the last three weeks.' He shook his head. 'I'd like to guess whoever's doing it feels they've exhausted this area and are moving somewhere else, because they sure were giving us a black eye. But that's too much to hope for. We have to figure they're laying low for some reason. Maybe they're changing their location or technique. Maybe there's a power struggle in the organisation. Maybe a lot of things. It'll probably flare up again soon. Meanwhile, we can do with the rest.'

'Meanwhile, I've given you a tip. If the Manilas aren't sacrosanct, you ought to at least charge Tony with violating the city ordinance against firing a gun within the city limits. Jack McGuire happens to be lucky he's alive.'

'All right, we can send a detective over to ask questions.'

'One of the questions ought to be the name of his doctor. Bullet wounds are supposed to be reported.'

'Sure,' Dan sighed. 'We can do all of those things. We can waste twenty hours of manpower on it. Tony Manila will claim he sprained his ankle. His doctor will say he sprained his ankle. His family will say he sprained his ankle. And there's no way in the world we can make him show us he doesn't have a bullet wound. No way in the world.'

'So, who says you've got to attack a guy's strength? Try his weakness.'

'Weakness? He's got one?'

'A girl. Her name is Shelly Polk. I think she'll crack if she's given a chance. And I think she knows where some of the bodies are buried.'

Dan wrote the name down. 'You got an address for her?'

'Yeah. The Manilas' home.'

'That's not going to make it easy to ask her questions.'

'Which is why they're keeping her there. Ma and Pa Manila don't like her, but Tony does. I think she's their weak link. And if there's family friction over the girl, prying her loose might not be as tough as you think.'

'Thanks for the tip,' Dan said solemnly. 'I wish we had the manpower to do all the things you think we should do.'

'Thanks for telling me you don't. You give me some ideas as to where to go from here.'

'Don't play fast and loose, Simon. Don't break any laws.'

'First things first, Dan. Tony Manila shot Jack McGuire, but he was aiming at me. And it's not his trigger finger that's crippled.'

'That's a pretty serious charge, Simon, claiming a guy like Tony Manila tried to kill you. You got a motive?'

'As I said, he doesn't like me poking into his business. And what he's doing about it indicates he's got something to hide.'

'Maybe you should stay out of his business.'

I got testy. 'What are you trying to say?'

'All right, all right. I didn't mean it like that.'

'Maybe you cops ought to look into his business too.'

'Bring us a reason and we will. But don't you go trying to take the law into your own hands, Simon. If you do, there's no way I can help you. You have to know that.'

'Of course I know that. And of course you know that I'm going to protect myself.' I started to leave and turned back. 'By the way, Dan, I understand that my business card was among Dana Doxey's effects. Is that right?'

He nodded. 'Yes, but it's nothing against you. We don't regard that as any kind of evidence. It doesn't even prove she knew you.'

'Yeah, yeah.' I waved that away. 'What I'm interested in is the condition of the card.'

'Condition?'

'Torn, battered, wrinkled, stained?'

'No, none of those things.'

'Had it been used as a toothpick?'

'What're you talking about?'

'Are the edges frayed—as if someone had picked their teeth with it?'

Dan scratched his neck. 'You want to see it?' he said at last. 'You can't touch it, but I can show it to you.' He went to the Personal Effects file, hunted for a bit and brought back a glassine envelope.

Inside was my business card, but it wasn't the one I'd given to Ben Schill, which he'd used on his teeth. This card was as fresh and clean as the ones in my wallet.

I walked out frowning. How had *that* found its way into Dana Doxey's purse?

CHAPTER TWENTY-SEVEN

Monday was the day of reckoning, when Leonard Wood wanted a satisfactory progress report. My task was to locate a girl by the name of Nerissa Claire because he thought it would help him get Carla Brent a reduced sentence for killing her husband. I mention this because the way this case was going, I could confuse that goal with getting even with Tony Manila, with getting a decent burial plot for Dana Doxey, with finding out who'd killed her and who'd killed Lemon Eyes, with finding out how Shelly Polk came to have a picture of her and Tony taken at least four months before she had appeared on the scene. And, in the background, this stolen-car ring seemed to mean something, but I didn't know what. None of it made sense, and I'm not making sense.

Monday morning isn't the best time of the

week, even if it's June and cloudy and the temperature is only 73°, even if you have a secretary like Eileen who can make a Monday sing. Not even she could warm my cockles that day. I hadn't slept, and I felt lousy. I felt so lousy I hadn't shaved. I stalked into the office with a gruff, 'Hello,' entered my sanctum sanctorum and thrust myself into my chair. The desk was clean and dusted, so there was nothing to glare at. I glared anyway.

Eileen came in with coffee, flavoured to my taste (the wretch), and set it in front of me. 'A hard day's night?' she said.

'I'm the world's lousiest detective.'

She opened my bottom drawer, the one with the brandy in it, poured an ounce into my coffee and put the bottle away. 'Try it again from the top,' she said. 'Surely, not the lousiest! Maybe second lousiest?'

'What do you know that I don't know?'

'All I know is that Leonard Wood has an appointment for ten o'clock, and you don't want to see him.'

'Does your horoscope say anything else?'

'Yes. It says you are going to see him!'

'Does it tell you what *you're* going to do?'

'No. It's a reluctant horoscope.'

'It's going to tell you to call the tax collector's office and ask for its assessed value on a Porsche belonging to a cop named Jake Metter.'

'I beg your pardon?'

'I want you to—'

'I know: call the tax collector's office and find out the assessed value on a Porsche belonging to a Jake Metter. Do I have it right?'

'You've got it right. If you have to identify Jake Metter, say he's a police officer.'

'A cop with a Porsche?'

'It's not the Porsche that matters, it's the value. Find out how much it's worth!'

'Yes, O Sacred Cow. Would you like more brandy?'

'Not with Leonard Wood in the same morning.'

She went her way and I went mine, and it was a good thing the bottle stayed in the drawer because Leonard Wood was on tap before I'd half finished what I had.

Eileen showed him in, I stood up to shake hands, and Eileen brought him an unspiked coffee. Leonard Wood only nodded in acceptance. He was assessing my appearance. He didn't look so good himself.

'I needn't ask,' he said at last, 'if you've been hard at work on my problem. The newspapers have been keeping me quite well informed. Your name was mentioned in connection with the murder of Dana Doxey, a go-go dancer at

253

Frank's Bar. Your name was mentioned in connection with the shooting of a priest outside the aforesaid bar. Am I right in assuming that these events are related to the search you are conducting for the individual I want found?'

I said he was correct in that assumption.

'I gather,' he continued, 'that, despite all this celebrity, you have not yet succeeded in locating this individual?'

'Nerissa Claire? No, I have not located her.'

His thick lips and broad mouth did not form into a smile. 'Have you made any progress in that direction?'

'I've come to a lot of dead ends, if you call that progress.'

'I don't.'

'I didn't think you would.'

'Do you think you will, in time, be able to locate her?'

'No.'

That at least got me an arched eyebrow. 'Why?'

'I think she's dead.'

He arched the other one. It was an idea that hadn't crossed his mind. 'You think she's dead?' He leaned toward me a few hair breadths. 'Why?'

'I don't have any evidence one way or the other. It's just a hunch.'

His jaundice-coloured face showed animation. The mouth worked, the eyes dilated. He was getting excited. 'Something,' he said, 'has happened to give you that hunch. Hunches don't come from God, they come from experience. How'd you get the hunch?'

'Ah, me,' I said. 'The legal mind. I don't analyse such feelings. I suppose, if I think about it, it's the sum total of a lot of things. First of all, Nerissa quits go-go dancing the same night her lover gets murdered by his jealous wife. Yet she has no way of knowing the wife is going to commit this act at that time. That's very funny.

'Second point. She not only quits, she disappears, and we find that she's turned her apartment over to a cousin who arrives in town to room with her at precisely the moment she decides to depart. That's pretty damned inhospitable, don't you think?'

'Yes,' he said in a waiting voice. 'I think I would concede that.'

'Nobody has seen or heard of Nerissa since. She dropped from sight without even leaving a splash. All trace lines reach dead ends. So, think about it, Leonard. You're a lawyer, you have a legal, analytical mind. What's more likely: that she's go-go dancing in Caesar's Palace, or she's lying in a cement coffin at the bottom of a nearby river?'

Leonard couldn't fault my rationale, even if he didn't like it. He had another rationale to go with it, though. 'But who would want to harm her?' he queried with a certain disbelief.

That's when Eileen strode quietly into the room, placed a piece of paper in front of me, and left again without a word. On the paper was written, 'Property Tax: Jake Metter Porsche—$18,000.'

I read it and breathed a little easier. All the ideas I'd been playing with through the wee hours last night were specs. No way could I put the pieces of this case together. The best I could do was relate half a dozen bits without contradiction, but that still had me out in left field. That's why I wanted to know the price of the Porsche. If it was high, there was a glimmer of light at the end of the tunnel.

I reached across the desk to hand the paper to Leonard. 'Read that.'

He did and handed it back. 'It doesn't mean anything to me. What do you want me to read it for?'

I smiled. I wasn't high enough in the catbird seat to grin. I smoothed the paper in front of me and said, 'I'm going to tell you a story. This is not a true story, because there are too many holes in it. This is a fairy story, which might hold an element of truth. Okay?'

He was paying for my time, so he said, 'Okay.'

'You're defending a woman named Carla Brent on charges of murdering her husband, who was a cop, right?'

'Right.'

'What did her husband do in the police department?'

'Do? He was a policeman. He did what policemen do—whatever that is—protect the public.'

'He held a particular position. Do you remember what it was?'

'He was the chief's personal secretary.'

'Which means all memos, all minutes of all meetings, all top-secret communications, all discussions of police-department procedures, problems, plans, methods, hopes, fears—all police department secrets—passed through his hands, right?'

'Yes, I suppose.'

'He wasn't a decision maker, but he knew the decisions. Right?'

'Yes, but what's this got to do with a jealous wife?'

'Nothing. That's the point. Let's talk about a hot-car ring that's been operating in this city the last six months, which has been driving the cops crazy. Have you heard about it?'

Wood shook his head.

'Every lead the cops get goes up in smoke. Every clue is a dead end. Every raid they pull gets them a handful of air. The cops are hog-tied. They're baffled.'

Leonard Wood sat straight in the chair. 'Is it your contention that this is because Matt Brent was privy to police-department secrets?'

'Let's at least think about the possibility. Let's start by considering his girl friend, a go-go dancer named Nerissa Claire. What's her background? Whom did she go with before she took up with Matt Brent?'

'I don't know.'

'Last October she went for a while with a guy named Tony Manila, whose family's in the car-servicing business—repairs, parking facilities, rentals, etcetera.'

A wary look came into Leonard's eyes. He listened more intently.

'That didn't last long. Next, she's seen with a cop named Jake Metter. That's a big come-down, right? From a rich, single young buck to a poor, old married cop?'

Leonard pressed his fingertips together. 'Tony threw her over?'

'Who knows? But now look what happens. Metter introduces her to another poor, old married cop—Matt Brent—and she and Matt go for each other in a big way. Sound funny?'

'Well, she was an attractive girl from what I understand. Lots of old married men lose their heads—'

'But what's he got to make her lose *her* head?'

Leonard Wood was cautious. 'Who knows a woman's mind?'

'Meanwhile, Jake Metter's left out in the cold. Does he mind? So far as I can make out, he goes back home to his wife.'

Wood pointed to the paper in front of me. 'You're saying when he went back to his wife, it was with an $18,000 Porsche?'

'It had to come from somewhere.'

'You're suggesting that Metter was paid to introduce Matt Brent to Nerissa Claire?'

'That would explain where the Porsche came from.'

'Do you have any evidence?'

'Of course not. This is a fairy story, remember?'

Wood inched forward in his chair. 'What's the rest of it?'

'Nerissa Claire is Mata Hari. She picks Matt's brains. She plays on his ego. He tells her all the secrets of the police department. Those that deal with the stolen-car ring—what the department's suspicions are, what their plans are, what they'll do next—she passes on to Tony Manila, who really didn't ditch her at all, merely planted her.'

'Do you have any evidence that the Manila family heads this stolen-car ring?'

'Nope. I said it's a fairy story.'

'But you say Nerissa's dead. Why would they kill her?'

'So she couldn't talk.'

'But why would she say anything. And why would they kill her after Carla shot Brent? What's the point?'

'The point might be that Carla didn't shoot Brent. Somebody else shot Matt Brent and Nerissa knew who it was.'

Leonard's eyes bugged out a half an inch. 'You're crazy,' he said. 'Everybody knows Carla Brent did it.'

'No,' I said. 'Everybody knows that Carla Brent has the world's lousiest alibi. That's all they know.'

'But if Carla didn't do it, who did?'

'I'd guess Tony Manila. He seems to be hit man for the family. Of course this is just a theory and, like all theories, it's got a lot of holes in it.'

Leonard tried to sort it out. 'You're saying Tony bribed the cop, Metter, to introduce Matt

Brent to Nerissa, and he bribed Nerissa to seduce Brent and give him a pipeline to all the police secrets so that Tony's family could operate a stolen-car ring without getting caught? Then Brent catches on or something, so Tony kills him and Nerissa to keep them from talking?'

'That's the general idea.'

'And you think Carla never shot her husband at all?'

'If my theory is correct.'

Leonard Wood sat back in his chair, pressed his long fingers together again and sighed, 'My, my, my, my. She told me to plead her innocent, and I was trying to get her to go for manslaughter. No wonder she hates me.'

'Don't go overboard, Leonard. It's still a fairy story. The only hook it hangs on is Metter's eighteen-thousand-dollar Porsche. If the tax office meant to say eight thousand dollars you can throw it out the window.'

Leonard was excited nevertheless. I'd opened up green pastures, and he didn't want the gates to shut. 'They wouldn't make a mistake like that,' he breathed. 'They wouldn't do that to me.'

I held up the slip of paper with the eighteen-thousand-dollar figure on it. 'Don't run wild. You know how far this would take you

261

in court, don't you?'

The answer was nowhere, but he wouldn't be stifled. 'It's a lead,' he said. 'We can build from there. Let's see, if Nerissa's dead, where would they bury her?'

'Not where you'll ever find her.'

He came down to earth, and he was on me, Abraham Lincoln serious. 'Listen Kaye, you've *got* to locate her. That's what's important.'

'I know. That's what you hired me to do. I'm telling you I don't think it can be done.'

'No, no, I mean I want you to find her body. Originally I wanted you to find her alive. Now I want you to find her dead.'

'There's no evidence that she *is* dead. I'm just giving you my best guess.'

'But you have to realize—finding her body will exonerate Carla. Listen to me, Kaye! She's *got* to be dead.'

I shook my head. 'Dammit, for a lawyer you should have stuck to clipping coupons. I told you this is a fairy story. This is not what happened. Some of it might have, but what did and what didn't, I don't know. Before you swan dive over Niagara, you'd better listen to what's wrong with that story. And if you can find a solution to what's wrong, then you can polish your gold star.

'First!' I held up a finger to silence him. 'There's a girl named Shelly Polk who knows a helluva lot more than she's saying. What she claims is that she's Nerissa's cousin, that she moved into Nerissa's condo on or about June first to hunt for a modelling career in our fair city. She moves in either the day before or the very day that Nerissa disappears. She has a phony story about where Nerissa went; she won't talk about Nerissa's background. In short, if she's Nerissa's cousin, I'm Simple Simon.

'What's more, this broad, who's supposedly just come to town, is Tony Manila's steady date from that day forward. Where did he meet her? How does she fit in?

'And I'll tell you something else. In her condo—the one Nerissa was paying the rent on—was a photo of her and Tony Manila taken not later than last winter because she's bundled to her chin and eyebrows in furs in front of a ski slope. This means Tony knew Shelly at least four months ago, and if Shelly and Nerissa fought over Tony, and Shelly won, Nerissa might have disappeared because she was in the way, not because she knew too much.'

'Well,' Wood said, protecting his investment, 'I think it's safe to say that of the two possibilities...'

263

'Then there's this little problem,' I continued. 'If my fairy story had really happened, where would we be? Let's think about that. Tony Manila kills Matt Brent because Matt has found out he's being used. Tony then kills Nerissa, who was nowhere near Matt's shooting, because she knew Tony's plan. Never mind the holes in that part of it, let us now consider the situation. Everything is fine, right? The stolen-car ring has to curtail activities until it can get another pipeline into the police department, but otherwise, the coast is clear. Matt and Nerissa are dead. Nobody's left who can expose the Manila family. All they have to do is sit tight. The town should be quiet, right?

'But it isn't quiet. First, a go-go dancer by the name of Dana Doxey is stabbed to death. One might think it an unrelated killing except that somebody points a finger at me by planting my business card in her purse.

'Second, Tony Manila gets violent because I try to talk to Shelly Polk. Why should he care?

'Third, neither Shelly nor Tony will say anything meaningful about what happened to Nerissa. That spells death to me, and I can understand that from Tony. But why is Shelly playing such a game? She's in this up to her pretty little neck, but she doesn't fit into my fairy tale.

'Lastly, Tony Manila tries to kill me. Why? What's he afraid—'

Leonard Wood sat up. 'You mean when the priest got shot...'

'He was protecting me.'

'You're in danger. This case—'

'Don't worry about it. It happens all the time. The point is, what's he after me for? What's he afraid of?' I kept up the chatter to get Leonard's mind off *non sequiturs* like my personal safety. 'I have to assume he stabbed Dana and that—' I stopped dead as the thought struck me.

He wasn't following *non sequiturs* now. He was leaning forward. 'What's the matter?'

I snapped my fingers. 'I don't assume he stabbed Dana. I *know* he did. That's how my card got into her purse. *He* put it there!'

'I don't know what you're talking—'

'Yes, yes. It was a clean card that was in her purse. The only cards I gave out were to Ben Schill, who picked his teeth with it, and to Mrs Oates, who gave it back, wet and smeared. So where did the clean card come from? It had to have been taken out of my wallet without my knowing it, and the only time that could have happened was after Tony sapped me in Shelly's apartment.'

265

I rubbed my chin. 'That's got to be it. He's the sonuvabitch who killed her. I know it as if I saw him do it. I owe him for that too. That's a double score I've got to settle with him.'

Leonard Wood watched me ruminate. 'Does that help?' he said. 'Does that tell you anything?'

I shook my head. 'That's the trouble. It doesn't fit. If he's killed Matt Brent and Nerissa Claire, what's he got to fear? What's he trying to keep us from discovering? He should be home free.'

The lawyer rose from the chair to his gaunt height. 'Solving problems like that is your business, Kaye, and I'm sure you'll find a way. What I like is your fairy story. If you can make it come true, I'll pay you ten thousand dollars. That's what it's worth to me if you can demonstrate to the satisfaction of the authorities that Carla Brent did not kill her husband. I don't care anymore if you find Nerissa Claire. I don't care if she's dead or alive. I don't care whether Tony Manila killed Matt Brent, or if it was somebody else. All I care is that you prove Carla didn't do it. Fair enough?'

Fair? I'd be going after Tony anyway, for Dana if nothing else. 'It won't be easy,' I said, 'but you've got a deal.'

CHAPTER TWENTY-EIGHT

Leonard and I dictated a proper contract for Eileen to type for our signatures, and it was close to noon when I saw him out the door. He was a happy man. He thought his problems were already solved. For the rich, life is simple. You pay money and your troubles go away.

Eileen looked happy, too. 'That'll take care of a lot of rent,' she said when the lawyer had gone. She was another who thought the money was already in the bank.

'I haven't earned it yet,' I reminded her.

'You will.'

It's nice to have a supportive secretary. It's good for the morale. But it doesn't solve any problems. 'Don't ask me how,' I said. 'Because I don't know.'

That was the trouble. I didn't know. Somehow I had to show that Tony Manila had killed Matt Brent. And what was there to go on that wasn't pure speculation? I wanted to get Tony. I needed to get him, in self-defence if nothing else, and never mind ten thousand dollars. But what was there to get him on?

I thought about it for a while. I thought about it through a sandwich in the coffee shop around the corner, and there wasn't much I could come up with that had an ironclad look to it. There wasn't much I could come up with that sounded as if it had possibilities.

Anyway, at ten after two, I took a flyer. I looked up Jake Metter's number in the phone book and dialled. It was his wife who answered. Jake was on duty. I asked when he'd be off duty, and she told me four o'clock and who was this speaking?

I didn't answer that. I said, in my Humphrey Bogart voice, 'You know that Porsche of his—that eighteen-thousand-dollar Porsche?'

'Eighteen thousand?' I could hear her gasp. 'But you're mistaken—'

I interrupted her. 'Tell your husband it's a stolen car. Do you get that? Tell him it's a stolen car.'

'Stolen?' She sounded frightened. 'He bought it second-hand. There must be some mistake.'

'Tell him,' I continued roughly, 'that it's going to come out that it's stolen, and when it does, he's through. You understand that? He's gonna be through!'

She was close to panic now. 'Please. Who are you? What do you mean "through"?'

'Just tell him he's through.' I hung up with a bang, sat back in my chair and contemplated the rest of my afternoon. Jake Metter would come home at four o'clock and get the message. If I was right about any of the facts in the case, he would get in touch with the Manila family and want to know what the hell the story was. That was supposed to be a brand new eighteen-thousand-dollar Porsche they'd given him. He'd feel like a boob if he'd accepted a stolen car with forged papers.

I took off at half-past three and fought traffic over to Metter's place, stashing the heap around a corner. I walked past the Metters' driveway, and the Porsche wasn't in sight. I didn't expect it to be. He'd have it hidden in the garage, free from rain and dust and, most important, theft. There was a big run on Porsches, and I figured it was fifty-fifty the Manilas really had paid him off with stolen goods. That would be a nice irony—like counterfeiters bribing the cops with counterfeit bills.

I didn't do my stake-out from the car. I kept that out of sight and watched the house from around a corner. It was sunny and hot. There were some kids in a neighbouring backyard, playing in bathing suits with a hose. A fat black woman with a heavy shopping bag came down the hill on flat feet. Seven miles overhead jets went by. Closer to the ground a barn swallow tried to drive another barn swallow off his turf.

Jake Metter came home at four thirty-five. He arrived on foot from the bus, made a military right face onto his walk, mounted the small porch and pushed open his front door. I returned to my car, climbed in and waited. If he went anywhere in the Porsche, he'd pass the end of my street.

It took exactly eight minutes. The Porsche shot by like the opening lap of the Indy 500. By the time I turned the corner, it was out of sight.

I picked it up at the straight stretch where Metter was waiting for a red light at the bus stop. There was nothing between us, and if he paid attention to his rearview mirror, he'd know I was behind him.

I drifted along slowly, and he was off and running while I was still two hundred feet away. I didn't try to keep up. He'd notice and start evasive action. Besides, I thought I knew where he was going—Manila's Garage, the biggest garage in town and a real showplace. If he went anywhere else, my theory was a bust, and I was in left field again. If he didn't go there, it didn't matter where he went.

Jake didn't disappoint me. He led me where

I thought he would, and he made himself easy to follow.

Manila's Garage is half a block long and a hundred feet deep. It's a five-storey brick box, built like an armoury, and occupies a spot halfway out Mattson Street where decay sets in. There're four islands of gas pumps outside the far half, with service doors and parking facilities on the near half. The parking facilities were Jake's target, and there was nothing cute or sly about his approach. He swung the car into the proper lane and disappeared inside where the elevators were.

That was half the ball game. Jake was running to the source to check on the legitimacy of his pride and joy. Vincent Manila owned the sonuvabitch. Vincent Manila also stole automobiles and Jake knew it. At least that's how I read it. A court of law was something else again.

I reined my heap in at a bus stop a block from the garage and pondered my next move. I didn't really want to walk into the place and ask for an audience—not all by my lonesome without even Eileen knowing where I was. On the other hand, sitting outside would gain me nothing. Jake might be chasing Vincent Manila around the office, demanding proof he wasn't a scapegoat. Or, for all I knew, he might merely be parking his car in Manila's Garage. Hundreds of people did it every day.

Advance, or hold back? It was a tough decision. It was a decision I never had to make. Thirty seconds after I'd put my wheels against the curb, a soft gloating voice, in the open window at my shoulder said, 'I thought you'd be tailing him,' and when I turned, I was looking into the dark, narrow, chrome-plated eye of Tony Manila. He had his right hand inside the lapel of his jacket where his shoulder holster was, and he was supporting himself awkwardly with a cane in his left.

Dumb me. I lay a trap to catch a cluck like Metter and forget the smart boys can read it and lay a trap of their own. I don't know that Tony was all that great in the brain department, but you have to figure the old man Vincent was. He wasn't running a successful stolen-car ring with peanut brittle inside his skull. Figure Vincent for the brains and Tony as the enforcer.

Right now, Enforcer Tony was enjoying life. There was that nice hot afternoon sun in a cloudless sky and me in his pocket. 'Hands on the wheel,' he said, reaching in my window to unlatch the back door. He opened it and climbed in.

'That's right,' he continued, making himself

comfortable and taking out his gun, keeping it low. 'So you want to know where Jake Metter's going, huh? Well, you shouldn't stop here. You should follow him.' He couldn't keep the rasp out of his voice any longer. 'Go on in the garage. Do what he did. And don't make one false move. I don't want to spill your guts all over the sidewalk.'

Tough Tony didn't leave me many options. There was plenty of traffic—it's a well-travelled thoroughfare—but that wouldn't stop him from putting a bullet through my brain and limping to the garage as calm as you please. If a passer-by noticed, which wasn't likely, he probably wouldn't know what was going on. And if he did, he wouldn't do anything but get out of there as fast as he could. The smart monkey says: keep your nose clean; see, hear and speak no evil.

I turned the key, shifted, and followed the path of the Porsche, making a right turn through the doors of the parking section. Inside, the only bright lights were in the checkout office. A curly haired, scrawny youth with black fingernails and a gimpy left leg crossed the exit ramp to give me a card. He jumped when Tony said, 'Take us to the top.'

'Hey, Mr Manila, I didn't see you.'

'Take us to the top, and that's right—you

didn't see me. You didn't see anything.'

'Yeah, sure.'

He limped to the elevator, and Tony made me inch the car along behind. We boarded, and the youth pulled the door rope and the heavy partitions came together from bottom and top. He punched the fifth floor button and we grumbled and growled upward. It was a slow ride, but not slow enough. In the time I had, I couldn't even begin to think of a way out.

At the top the kid opened the doors, and Tony warned him again to keep his mouth shut. He made me drive off the stage and park in the nearest slot. When we got out, the kid had closed the doors, and the elevator was grinding its way downstairs again. That left us alone together, just Tony and me. And Tony was crippled. He had to hold the cane with his right hand to ease the weight on his leg, so he held the gun southpaw, which wasn't his shooting hand. It did me no good, though, because he made me keep my hands on my head and walk ten feet in front.

We went through a fire door that said No Admittance. Beyond was a green-carpeted hall lined with pink flowered wallpaper.

There was an exit door at the end, and a door with Private on it halfway down. 'Knock on it,' Tony told me, switching the gun to the proper hand.

I gave the door a couple of raps, and Vincent Manila opened it. 'Yeah,' he said, 'I was expecting you.' He stepped back to let me in.

It was a large office with electric-blue carpeting and lots of chrome furniture: couches, chairs, a couple of desks and a sink by the cabinets at the right-hand end. Facing me were windows to the street, a wall full of them. On the left was a door to private areas.

Standing behind the short, grey, stocky Vincent, was Jake Metter. He was by the windows, and his jaw sagged when he saw who I was. 'What the hell is he doing here?' he said to Vincent and clutched the back of a chair. 'Do you know what the hell you're doing?' His face was wild.

'Stuff it,' Vincent said. He ran his hands over me, removed my gun and put it in his own pocket. In back of me, Tony limped in and shut the door.

Jake's eyes darted from me to Vincent to Tony. 'For Chrissake,' he said, 'you're outta your mind letting him come in here like this!'

'Why?' Vincent said. 'He knows you know us. Sit down, Kaye. Be comfortable.'

I said thanks, but I'd rather stand. That caught me a clout from Tony's gun, which felled me into the chair, and I lay there, half on the floor, trying to remember who I was.

In the distance, Metter's voice said, 'What do you mean, he knows? How *could* he know?'

Vincent went around and sat behind his desk. 'That's what we brought him up here to find out. That, and what else he knows.'

'The sonuvabitch,' Jake said in sudden rage. 'I'll beat it outta him myself.'

'Be my guest,' Vincent said. He looked at me appraisingly. 'That's pretty cute, phoning Jake's wife that his Porsche is hot.'

'*He* did that?' Jake cried out. 'How did you know?'

Vincent smiled dryly. 'Because your Porsche isn't stolen. So when you call me about the message you got, I have to wonder who's trying to make trouble and why? Since Mr Kaye is the only troublemaker around, it's not hard to decide he made the call. As to why he made the call, the obvious reason was to panic you and see where you'd run. So you ran to us, which is what he wanted to find out.'

Metter's voice was a shriek. 'Then why the hell did you tell me to come here? Why didn't you tell me to stay home?'

'Because we've been wanting to have a little talk with Mr Kaye for some time, and we thought that this might be the way to arrange it.' Vincent gave Metter an encouraging smile.

'Now do you see?'

Metter paced a little and rubbed his forehead. 'But now you've given the show away. Now he knows too much.'

'That he does,' Vincent agreed, 'but I suspect that he knew it before now. And that's what I want to discuss with Mr Kaye: how much he knows and who else knows it.' He grew bored with Metter and turned to me. 'I trust you've been listening to all this, Mr Kaye, so its not necessary for me to repeat it?'

I struggled to straighten myself in the chair. 'I don't really know anything,' I grunted. 'I was hired to find Nerissa Claire, and I haven't even been able to do that.'

Vincent said smoothly, 'You're certain of that, are you?'

'That's right. Your son Tony can back me up. He made sure I didn't find out anything.'

Vincent filled a glass from a water flagon on his desk, took a pill from a small box from a drawer, put the pill on his tongue and washed it down his throat. He took his time, and he looked like an actor in a TV commercial playing up to the camera. And we watched with the fascination of a bird for a snake. Nobody said a word.

Vincent carefully replaced the glass on the tray with the flagon. He said, 'You're very

277

modest, Mr Kaye. You're much too modest. You would like us all to believe that you've been working on a case for one whole week and you haven't been able to find out a single thing? We know how good a detective you are, and we know better than to believe something ridiculous like that. A detective as good as you are is going to find out a very great deal in a week.' His voice hardened. 'There's not going to be any question about that. For instance, I think you know why my son has to use a cane today. And, of course, there's the phone call you made to Mrs Metter. I think you had an idea where Jake would run. And I'd like to know what gave you that idea. Would you like to confide in us, here in the comfort of this office?' He waved at the cabinet beside the sink. 'Would a drink free your tongue? I have a well-stocked bar.'

I said, 'Really, you flatter me. My ignorance is quite astounding.'

'As I thought,' Vincent sighed. He glanced at Metter. 'You wished for the chance to persuade him, Jake. You may commence at will.'

I'm not going to say Jake Metter leaked the milk of human kindness when he drooled, and I knew he ached to put his fist through my face. I also suspect that he was one of the cops on the force who worked over uncooperative suspects down in the bowels of the police building—suspects who'd be afraid to squeal. But he didn't want to molest me in front of a couple of hoods and on their orders. That irrevocably put him on their side, and I'd know it. He waved away Vincent's offer. 'That's all right, forget it.'

Vincent wasn't about to forget it. 'Oh, but I insist. I'd like to see how you cops get confessions. I can learn much.'

'We don't get confessions that way, Mr Manila. It's not legal.'

'Look, I don't want to argue with you,' Vincent said, his tone sharpening. 'I want you to make him talk. If you can do it without leaving marks, do so by all means. However, if you have to get his blood all over the carpet, don't give it a thought. I'll replace it tomorrow.'

Metter was finding out what pressure was. 'Listen, I think it'd be better if I didn't appear in this...'

'But you're going to appear, Metter. You are in possession of a very expensive car which, I believe, you want to keep. In fact, I believe it's vital that you keep it. Because if you didn't, the fact that it's worth eighteen thousand dollars would immediately come out. And where would you get eighteen thousand dollars —legitimately? Think about it. Where would

you? If the police commission put that question to you, what would you answer? You not
only would lose your car, you'd go to jail, too.'

Metter worked his mouth. 'And what's going
to happen when he leaves here? What's *he*
going to say?'

Vincent gave both of us a very cold smile.
'I don't really think Mr Kaye plans to say
anything about anything. Am I not right, Mr
Kaye?'

'You're right,' I said. 'You can tell Jake to
have it engraved on my tombstone: 'Vincent
Manila was right. Simon didn't talk.'

Jake had to know I was going to be killed,
but he wouldn't admit it. As long as it happened outside his ken, he could accept it. But I
was thrusting it at him. He was going to
become involved with my fate, unwelcome
as it might be.

'Well, now listen,' he said, like a little boy
hopping from one leg to the other, 'I've got to
get going. All I wanted was assurance that the
car's on the level. I earned it, you know. So
now I'd better—'

He started around my chair for the door, but
Vincent's voice stopped him. 'Metter,' it snapped, 'do you know what's going to happen to
you if you go out that door?'

Metter stared with a sick look on his face.

Vincent drew his finger across his throat and uttered a rasping sound. 'You're broken, Metter. You're going to lose everything you've got and you're going to jail. Think about that, Metter!'

'But I've done for you,' Metter said. 'I've earned everything you paid me. We're even. We can call it quits.'

Vincent shook his head. 'There's no such thing as quits. I thought you knew that. I thought you were smart enough to know that. When you're bought, you stay bought. Now, do you want to do what you're told and make this bastard, Kaye, tell us what we want to know, or do you want Tony to do it and you walk out and call it quits?'

Metter turned and went back to the window. He looked blankly through the panes, then sighed and faced us. 'I'll do it,' he said.

CHAPTER TWENTY-NINE

Jake moved slowly my way, and I rose just as slowly. My fists were doubled, and I braced my feet. Jake hesitated. He was big, but I was better conditioned than he. I was better all-around than he.

Vincent Manila took my gun from his pocket and aimed it my way. 'Okay, tin hero,' he said. 'Sit down.'

'Make me.'

'If this gun of yours goes off, you're gonna lie down. They're gonna plant you under a blanket of flowers.'

'So shoot me. Because if this punk takes one more step forward, I'm going to throw him through the window.'

Vincent was stymied. The gun was steady enough, but his options were gone. Death is the ultimate threat, and if you can't frighten somebody with that, you've got nothing.

Tony, however, didn't deal in such subtleties. He whacked me from behind with his own gun, and I was out before I hit the floor.

I don't know how long the curtain of darkness left me in limbo, but when I came to, I found myself on the electric-blue carpet, lying where I'd fallen, and the only difference was that my hands were now cuffed in front of me.

I wasn't on the floor long. The second my eyelids flickered, Tony and Jake got me under the armpits and threw me into the chair.

Then Jake was in front of me, resurrecting all the hatred he'd developed over the past week. 'You're gonna talk, you sonuvabitch!' His snarl was geared to make a good impression on the Manilas, father and son. Next he tried to kick me in the groin. I twisted enough to take the blow where it hurt like hell, but nothing like it would have hurt. 'You're gonna tell us everything we want to hear,' he went on, 'because I'm gonna give you a going-over until you do.'

'Some hero,' I grunted. 'Sure, you can let them kill me, but how could you sit on your ass when they kill another cop?'

He gave me a whack across the side of the head, which felt as if it split my skull. The room went reeling. 'You don't talk sense, but you're damned well going to.'

'Tony killed Matt Brent,' I shouted at him, calling him a few censored names as well. 'And you kiss the blood off his hands.'

That stopped him for a second. It stopped all of them. Jake took one look at Tony and maybe he was afraid of what he saw, for he wheeled back on me. 'That's a lie,' he yelled. 'Carla killed Matt. His wife killed him.'

'She was framed,' I yelled back. 'What would she kill him for? Tony did it. Matt got wise to how Nerissa was using him. He was going to blow the whistle. Tony blasted him to shut him up.'

Tony let fly at me with a gun in his fist, but Metter caught his arm and threw him back. Metter's brow was clouded. He didn't believe me, but I made enough sense for him to want to hear more. 'Hold it,' he snapped. 'What's this guy talking about?'

I didn't let the others answer. 'I'm talking about you,' I blurted out. 'You introduced Nerissa to Matt. You set it up so she could pick his brains. And when he catches on and Tony offs him, that makes you responsible. You caused Matt Brent's death. That eighteen-thousand-pound white Porsche you drive has Matt Brent's blood on it. You didn't just support a hot-car ring for that Porsche, you killed a fellow cop for it.'

Metter turned uncertainly to the Manilas. 'Did Brent get wise?'

Tony said smoothly, 'Matt Brent knew from

nothing. Don't listen to this guy. Can't you see he's desperate? Brent's wife killed the stupid jerk. Even her own lawyer knows that.'

Jake flared. 'He wasn't a stupid jerk. He was a good cop.'

'He was a sucker for a skirt. His wife had it in for him, not me. Ask Nerissa if you don't believe me.'

I said to Metter, 'You can't ask Nerissa. Nerissa's dead. Tony killed her so she couldn't talk.'

Tony looked at Metter and then at me. 'Oh,' he said. 'So I killed Nerissa? That's to keep her from talking, huh?' He turned. 'When did you last see Nerissa, Jake? How dead was she?'

'Not dead at all.'

'You want to ask her if I killed Matt?'

'Forget it. This creep's just trying to cause trouble.'

'Then go to work on him—find out what he knows, not what he tries to make you believe.'

Jake Metter turned to me, and his face was purple. 'You had me going, you sonuvabitch. You almost made me buy it—that Tony killed Matt. You're clever. That's one thing I'll say— you're clever. But nobody makes a sucker out of Jake Metter, mister. That's a no-no, and you're gonna bleed for it. I don't know how much pain you've ever suffered before, but you're

285

gonna suffer now like nobody's suffered.'

He turned to Vincent and Tony. 'You got any more information you want out of him along the way?'

Vincent said, 'Work him over. We'll think about it while we watch.'

Tony said, 'Just don't kill him. We want to take him out of here alive.'

'You think I'm a jerk? I don't commit murder for anybody.'

Vincent said, 'Don't knock him out. We don't want to waste time waking him up.'

'Don't worry,' Metter said. 'The art of torture is to keep the pain level just short of the limits the subject can endure without passing out. The other restriction—in the police business—is leaving marks. It's a fine art, inflicting pain without leaving marks.'

He looked me over with anticipation. I'd almost made him lose his eighteen-thousand-dollar Porsche. I'd almost cost him his job, his liberty, his pursuit of happiness. And there were a few old scores he had to settle with me, too. He'd be a long time sating himself on my pain.

'Can't help leaving marks with my fists,' he mused. 'But when we turn him loose, there's nobody he can cry to. Because nobody but us is gonna see what happens to him.'

286

'That's right,' Vincent said. 'He ain't gonna cry.'

It was the end of the line, but there was no point in holding still. The more trouble I could make, the better. So I didn't sit passively in my chair with my hands cuffed in front of me and prepare to deal with pain. I waited till Metter came close enough to throw his first punch, and then I sprang at him. What I did was swing both hands, heel first, like swinging a mallet. If I could have caught him right, I'd have broken his jaw, maybe even his neck. But, of course, you don't very often land a sucker punch, even if the other guy isn't expecting it, and Metter had enough wit and speed to half block the blow and duck. The result was that I knocked him to the floor, but I didn't knock him cold.

In fact, I didn't even stagger him. He rolled over and was on his feet like a cat—like a slow, out-of-shape cat. But it was fast enough. I couldn't follow up the advantage, not that it would have done me much good, what with two guns against me on the sidelines.

Metter retaliated with a couple of wild punches of his own, and he wasn't being a skilful torturer about it. He was a wounded bull charging a red cape.

I rode two high hard ones and tried to get

my cuffed arms over his head. We fell into my chair, him on top, me trying to bring up my knee.

Then the door at the end of the room opened, and a female voice let out a startled shriek and said, 'What are you doing? Whatever are you doing?'

It was Shelly Polk.

CHAPTER THIRTY

Everybody froze. It was like stop-action in the middle of a saloon brawl in a movie western—blurred cuspidors in midair, bottles half broken on cowboys' heads. And all because a young and very pretty girl, with an armful of packages, opened the door and walked in on a man's world where men were doing the sort of thing they don't do in front of ladies. It was like cutting out the four-letter words when the dowager walked in.

Tony stiffened and stepped in front of us. Vincent, behind the desk, took the delight out of his eyes. Jake Metter got to his feet and brushed himself off. I got to my own feet and stepped to the side. It was a reprieve, and I wanted room to manoeuvre.

She looked around at the group, sorting us out. 'Jake,' she said and frowned. 'What're you doing here? And Simon Kaye?' She saw the handcuffs and looked to Tony. 'How did he get here? I thought you didn't like him.'

Vincent's face went an off-shade of purple. 'Shut the hell up, big mouth,' he said to her. 'Get the hell out.'

Tony wheeled on him. 'Don't you talk to her like that. She can stay if she wants.' He beckoned. 'Come on in, honey. We're just having a meeting.' He smiled fondly. 'You been shopping?'

'Yeah,' she said uncertainly. 'Like you said to.' She wanted to leave, but he hadn't told her to go. 'I bought a lot of things.'

He looked at the boxes she carried. 'Aw, that ain't enough. I told you to *shop*.'

'It's all right. There's a lot more. They're going to deliver.'

'That a new dress? Let's see it.'

She was extremely uncomfortable, and her eyes kept darting. Nevertheless, she obediently put the boxes down and displayed herself. The dress was a cool and airy summer print that made her look both saucy and sexy. She swung around slowly, uneasily. Tony licked his lips.

'Yeah, baby. It's got everything.'

Tony's father said, 'Yeah, it's great. Now go home. We got business.'

Tony got angry again. 'Stop insulting her, pa. Stop telling her what to do.'

'Then you tell her! Tell her to get her ass outa here.'

'And don't you tell me what to tell my girl. She can stay if she wants.'

'Yeah, sure, stay,' Vincent told her. 'Sit down. We're only gonna beat up a guy. Sit down and watch. You've seen it all before.'

'Knock it off, pa. Will ya knock it off?'

I figured it was time to say my piece. 'Sit down and enjoy it,' I encouraged. 'We're only having a discussion about how Tony here killed a cop named Matt Brent. Isn't that right, Tony?'

Tony called me a few names not meant for dowagers' ears.

Shelly looked at me tentatively. 'But Tony wouldn't kill somebody like Matt. He wouldn't have any reason.' She turned his way. 'Isn't that right, Tony?'

'Yeah,' Tony said. 'That's what I been telling the jerk.'

I blinked and my mouth opened. She had called him Matt! She didn't say, 'Who're you talking about?' She didn't even say, 'Matt Brent, the cop?' She said 'Matt,' and suddenly all the pieces fell into place.

'That picture!' I said to her. 'I should have guessed by the picture.'

'Picture?'

'You and Tony, in ski outfits, taken last winter!'

She gave me a blank look. I was talking off the wall. 'Picture,' I repeated. 'The hood covered your hair, and I took it for granted the hair was blond.' I gestured with my cuffed hands. 'But it wasn't blond back then. It was brunette, and Jake is right. Nerissa Claire isn't dead, and she didn't disappear. All you did was dye your hair and call yourself Shelly Polk.'

She looked from me to Tony. 'Hey, he's wrong, isn't he? Don't I tell him he's wrong?'

'Tell him he's out of his cotton-picking mind.'

'You're out of your cotton-picking mind.'

I turned to Jake Metter. 'That's why Tony killed Dana Doxey. Because the moment she saw Shelly Polk, she'd know it was Nerissa, and Nerissa wasn't supposed to be around. I knew he killed Dana, but I didn't know why.'

'What are you talking about?' Nerissa cried. 'Tony didn't kill Dana.'

'He stabbed her to death to keep her from

identifying you. He killed her over you.'

'Stop saying that,' she shrieked. 'Stop saying he killed Dana. Tony might have killed Matt, but he wouldn't kill Dana. She was a friend of mine.' Nerissa turned to him. 'You wouldn't kill Dana, would you, Tony?'

I kept going. 'And the young guy who worshipped Dana. He knew who killed her, and he was going to get even, but Tony killed him first. And then Tony tried to kill me. He tried to kill everybody who got close to you. He didn't want you found out. Why was that, Nerissa? Was he afraid you'd talk?'

She shook me away. It was Tony she was after. 'Tony, tell me you didn't kill Dana... not Dana. You never said you'd kill Dana.'

Tony was unnerved. He licked his lips uncertainly. But Tony didn't matter. Vincent was the one in control. He had a gun in his hand—my gun. 'Shut up, you bitch,' he snarled and wheeled on Tony. 'I told you to get rid of her. I told you and told you! You don't ever let anybody know too much and *live*!' (all of which said a great deal about the future of us in that room).

Tony was flustered, but Metter wasn't. 'You sonuvabitch,' he said to him. 'It wasn't Carla who killed Matt Brent. It was you?' He said to Nerissa, 'Is that right? *He* did it?'

She nodded, stricken. 'That's why he made me go into hiding. So I couldn't tell anybody. He was afraid I couldn't keep quiet.'

Vincent waved his gun at her, cursing Tony in a rage. 'Listen to her! Listen to her! I told you she's a sieve. I told you what to do to her. I told you to kill her. But you had to be cute. You had to fall for her. You had to protect her!'

Now it was Jake Metter. 'Matt Brent was my pal,' he shouted at Tony, drawing his own gun. 'You killed my pal!'

Tony's gun was holstered and he was helpless. He backed off a step, holding up his hands. 'Wait,' he cried.

Nobody waited. The room exploded in violence, everything happening at once. Vincent swung on Jake and blasted him with my gun. They were ten feet apart, with me closer, and even with the windows open, it sounded like dynamite.

Nerissa screamed and Jake shuddered. It was a mortal wound, but Vincent was too late. Jake was already pulling the trigger, and the sound of his gun rode on top of Vincent's blast, Tony was the target and he took a heavy hit in the upper body, not the heart, but close enough.

Tony fell, kicking and squirming, onto the couch by the windows, one hand clawing at the starting stain on his shirt, the other groping for his own gun. Jake, his knees sagging, mouth open and jaw hanging, tried to turn his gun on Vincent.

Vincent gave him a second shot, this time in the face, and a spray of blood exploded from his head like a fireworks display.

Jake dropped the gun and went backward, knocking over a chair. Nerissa, screaming, ran from him to the desk.

The sound of explosions stopped. There was nothing now but the aftersmell hanging in the air—that and Nerissa's screams. Three of us were upright, I a pace to the right of Jake's body, Nerissa beside the desk, Vincent, with unwavering gun, behind it. On the couch, stricken Tony was holding his gun laxly, clutching his wound, breathing stentorously, his dark eyes glowing with a dull, piercing, laser-like light. But never mind Tony. Vincent was the man with the active gun. He was the one who was running amok, and there was no place for Nerissa and me to hide.

I didn't move and the gun didn't come my way. He wasn't thinking about me. His sky was falling and he didn't know what to do. He turned to Tony. 'Why did you do it?' he cried out. 'Why did you let her live?'

'He shot me,' Tony muttered, staring at the dead cop. He called Jake ugly names and coughed up blood. He cursed and coughed up more blood. He was getting weak. Nerissa gaped at him, watching the blood spread, her shrieks still keening.

Vincent ogled the spreading stain, the blood erupting from Tony's mouth. He uttered a cry of pain. 'It's her,' he yelled, pointing a wild finger at Nerissa, who stopped in mid-shriek as suddenly as if somebody had cut off the audio.

'It's her!' Vincent yelled again. 'She killed you! She killed my son!' He dropped my gun on his desk and seized the terrified girl, ripping her dress down to the waist like an Iowan farmer husking corn.

My eyes were on the gun he'd discarded, but there was no way I could beat him to it. Nearer was Jake Metter's gun, lying half under his body. That wasn't a good risk either, but I moved a step closer.

At the desk Vincent was stripping the girl, tearing at her in a frenzy, his nails making blood streaks on her arms and body. She screamed and struggled, her voice shrill enough to shatter glass.

Underneath the dress she was wearing one of those frail, see-through bras that's next to wearing nothing at all. He ripped that from her like tissue paper. He was a tiger, and this time he left claw marks across her breasts.

'For this slut you should die?' the old man yelled at his son. 'For these tits you should die?' He sobbed. 'I told you to kill her. You knew she'd crack and talk. I told you and told you. But you had to keep her. You had to keep this slut.'

I was close enough now to grab Metter's gun in one dive, but it was still a losing proposition. Vincent was wild, but he wasn't deranged. He hadn't let the situation slip out of control. He could plug me with my own gun before I could get Metter's.

Now he tore off the rest of Nerissa's dress and flung it away. 'Clothes! Fancy clothes!' he yelled at Tony. 'You buy and buy. You should have killed her.'

The dress fell onto Jake's body, covering his gun. The old man was sobbing now. 'I should have killed her myself. Now she's killed you. I kill her now, but it's too late. But I kill her. I get even. I kill. I kill.' He reached for my gun.

That ended all arguments. I dove for Metter's revolver as Vincent picked up mine. I pushed the dress aside but had trouble getting my hands on the grip and trigger guard. The cuffs were hampering me. The old man paid no heed. He had the bleeding, terrified girl by the arm, my gun was in his hand, and he was screaming curses at her. I aimed Jake's gun at him, but Nerissa was in my way.

And that was the moment tough Tony, dying Tony, let his old man have a slug through the temple. Nobody was going to hurt his girl.

Blood and brains burst out the other side of Vincent's head and sprayed all over Nerissa. She jumped and screamed. Then she saw Tony swing the gun my way. She tried to get to me first. 'No, no,' she cried out. 'For God's sake. Don't kill any more.' She was sobbing and stumbling, trying to throw herself in front of me.

She wasn't going to make it, but it didn't matter. I had a gun now and Tony was wide open. I let him have it, one—two—three. It would have been four and five as well, except that Tony was dead before I even got to three. Three was for good measure.

CHAPTER THIRTY-ONE

Nerissa clung to me, hanging on my neck and sobbing like a child. She was spattered with blood, brains and hair, she had been roughly scratched, and some of the blood was her own. She was dressed in her underpants and she was a mess, but all she knew was she wouldn't look at the violence and mayhem that had taken place in the room.

I tried to pat her, but I couldn't with my hands cuffed. Instead, I made soothing noises and inched my way to Jake's body. They were his cuffs and I needed his keys. Nerissa wouldn't let go, and I dragged her with me.

'I never loved him. I was afraid of him,' she kept sobbing. 'I was afraid of his father. His father hated me.'

I fumbled through Jake's pockets until I got his key ring. Nerissa finally released me, and knelt, her hands between her knees, staring into my face with teary eyes, not looking at the body I was searching, not looking anywhere else, keeping herself together by watching me—and talking.

And could she talk! No wonder old Vincent had wanted her destroyed. She'd spill her guts to the first guy who asked her. She's a disaster in a business requiring an oath of silence. But you look at her body—well, at the moment you should give her a bath first—and you could see Tony's point of view. He wouldn't want her mouldering in a grave. He wouldn't even want her out of the state somewhere. He'd keep her where he could put his hands on her. He might use her as bait for Matt Brent, but he'd keep her for himself in between.

And now she was singing the story to me, and it came out like grand opera, with all the details and nuances and shadings, all about how she came to town with big modelling ideas and how she followed Dana into go-go dancing in a crummy downtown bar under the tutelage of a lascivious entrepreneur.

Then Tony took an interest in her, and she was the envy of the other girls, for he had dough and gave her things. Some of the things he gave her weren't so enviable—black eyes, one time cracked ribs. That was when she didn't want to seduce and betray Matt Brent. After she acceded to the request, she didn't get beaten anymore.

It was Tony who decided, from the reports

she brought him, that Matt had grown suspicious and had to be destroyed. It was Tony who told her the night to quit her job—the night he took Matt out of circulation. He gave her a new name and the story to tell, and ordered her not to discuss anything. 'Say what I told you to say and then shut up,' was the admonition he kept giving her, and he was going to kick out her teeth if she disobeyed.

'He really loved me,' she said with great earnestness. 'But he was scared. That's why he beat me. He was scared of his father, and they were both scared I'd spill the beans. I'm just no good at keeping secrets.'

'Sure he loved you,' I said. 'When was the last time you were treated with tenderness?'

'Tenderness? What's that?'

I looked at the marks where Vincent had bloodied her. They stood out against the spatterings, and I traced some of the less erotic ones and shook my head. 'Maybe I shouldn't ask why you ask. Ben Schill, Tony, Tony's father. Tell me—how did Matt Brent treat you?'

She shook her head. 'Would you believe, I don't even remember? I don't even remember what he looked like.'

There's a nice farewell to a dead cop.

I took her by the arms. 'I have to tell you something. You tried to save my life. You tried to get between me and Tony's gun. That was very brave.'

'It wasn't brave. He'd never have shot me.'

'It was very brave but very foolish, and I thank you.'

She said, still staring only at my eyes, 'I don't know you, I think maybe I do, but I really don't. But I'd rather save your life than Tony's. All he ever did was hurt people. Do you hurt people?'

'Yes, I hurt people.'

'I don't believe you.'

'Look behind you. Tony's lying there on the couch. I just shot him three times.'

She shook her head. 'I don't want to look at Tony. I'm glad he's dead. You know something? I can't remember his face anymore.' She put her hands on my arms. 'Can you take me away from here? Can I go away and never have to look at them anymore?'

'I'll take you away,' I said. 'I have to wash you off and find some clothes for you...'

'There's another dress in that box over there. I could put that on.' Her eyes brightened a little. 'Where will you take me?'

I got up and lifted her to her feet. 'You're going to have to talk to the police first,' I said. 'You're going to have to tell them what happened here, and what was going on before.'

'Do I have to memorize more stories, like with Tony? I always break down in the end and tell the truth.'

'That's all you have to do—tell the truth.'

'I guess I could do that all right. Would you go with me to the police? Could I hold onto your hand?'

I said I couldn't go with her, but my lawyer would. I'd call him now and, after he got here, we'd call the police.

She said, 'Can I wash up now and put on the other dress...and can I call you Simon?'

CHAPTER THIRTY-TWO

I didn't see Jack McGuire until the following evening. He was ambulatory, meaning they were sitting him up and making him walk. Right then he was in a chair by the window, wrapped in a dressing gown with a robe over his legs.

I told him why he got shot, which meant explaining everything that had happened, from Matt Brent's murder and Carla's arrest to my involvement, Dana's subsequent murder, and

302

finally, the wild West shoot-'em-up-type denouement that had taken place in Manila's garage. I ended by saying we no longer needed a cemetery plot for Dana Doxey. Nerissa had learned her background when they roomed together, so her parents had been contacted and the body was going west.

Jack said, 'And you killed Tony Manila? Tell me—because I'm really curious—how does it feel to kill a man?'

'I didn't really kill him,' I said. 'He was dying anyway. I just hastened the process a little.'

'Nevertheless, it was your bullet that did it. We all are going to die eventually, so the only thing that killing does is hasten the process a little.'

'All right,' I said. 'You want to know how it felt to kill Tony? It felt *good*! G-O-O-D. Good, good, good.'

Jack sighed. 'I hope the Lord will pretend he didn't hear that.'

'I'm sure he won't judge me any more harshly than you will. There is such a thing as justifiable homicide.'

'What about Carla Brent? Are they going to let her out of jail?'

'She's out. Leonard Wood was in a huddle with the D.A first thing this morning. He had

303

her out of there before noon. Of course, I don't know what she's got to go back to, but whatever it is, she's back to it. As for Leonard Wood, he's walking on air. He thinks I'm the greatest detective since the Hardy Boys.'

'I hope he backed it up with a cheque.'

'Paid in full, with a five-thousand-dollar bonus.'

'All's well that ends well, eh?'

'That says it.'

'But we're forgetting somebody.' He gave me one of those not-so-happy-ending smiles. 'What about Nerissa? What's going to happen to her?'

I was ready for him. 'Right now she's in my lawyer's care. He called me late this afternoon. She was still with the police, still telling them things. She's blown that stolen-car ring sky high. But no charges are going to be levelled against her.'

'She's lucky.'

'No, my lawyer's damned good.'

'And what's going to become of her after that, after she's let go? What's going to be the end of her story? Is it going to be happy, too?'

'I don't know what her story is. She hasn't told me her plans.'

'Find out, will you? You've left me in the

304

middle of a soap opera. Does she go back to home and family? Does she go back to go-go dancing? Does she end up as a *Playboy* centrefold?'

'She's probably going to go to jail as a material witness until after the trial...so she can't disappear again.'

'And what about you? You killed Tony. Do you go to jail too?'

'No. I'm free on my own recognizance.' I laughed. 'I said *you'd* produce me.'

'No self-respecting D.A would believe that.'

'It doesn't matter. I told you I've got a smart lawyer. He's paid to keep me out of jail.'

Jack shook his head. 'Simon,' he sighed, 'I have a feeling that one day one of the bodies I'm going to have to say prayers over is going to be yours. Do you ever think about that?'

'Sure I do. Last Saturday night! I was saying prayers over you. You were lying there on the sidewalk, and that sonuvabitch, Tony—at least I put a bullet through his leg!'

Jack said, 'Get out of here, will you? I want to pray for you, and if you're in the way, God's going to get nothing but static.'

I said, 'Say a kind word for Nerissa and Dana,' and left.

So it was back to the condo—my empty, gloomy

condo. Most of the time I like it that way. It's my nest, my retreat, my haven, my security blanket. Now and then, though, it can be my hellhole, the last desperate place on earth. Generally I like being alone. Once in a while, though, like now—leaving a crippled Jack Mc-Guire, leaving all that I knew of humanity behind, retreating to empty quarters with nothing for company but the frolic of TV, which is emptiness itself—the process can be agonizing.

So I parked the car and slowly shuffled up the stairs to the storm porch outside my condo door. It was grey-dark now, about nine o'clock.

And there she was, sitting on my top step, in a play-type dress, hugging her shins, her chin to her knees, waiting for me. Nerissa Claire.

I couldn't think of anything smart to say, so I said, 'Why aren't you in jail?'

She said, 'Your lawyer talked them out of it. He said something about recognizance— about *your* recognizance—that you'd be responsible for me.'

'The sonuvabitch!'

'He said I had to stay with you, that you have to be responsible for me until the trial.' She looked at the shock in my eyes and tears came to hers. 'I won't get in the way,' she said. 'If you want me to go somewhere else, I will. I'm used to doing what I'm told.'

'Oh, for Christ's sake!'

She wouldn't cry. 'Where do you want me to go?' she asked. 'I'll go.'

'Forget it.' I stepped over her and put my key in the door. 'Come on, on your feet. You can stay here. We might as well be lonely together.'

She got up and followed me inside. 'Will you teach me about tenderness?' she asked. 'Your lawyer said you're a tenderhearted sucker.'